THE IMPOSTER

ALSO BY ADRIANE LEIGH

Psychological Suspense

The Influencer

The Imposter

The Intruder

The Guests

She Let Me In

The Perfect Escape

The Last Writer

My Perfect Family

Contemporary Romance

From Salt to Skye

About That Summer

The Morning After

Confessed

Wild

Beautiful Burn

An Arrogant Gentleman

Written as Aria Cole

The Lumberjack's Bride

The Cowboy's Claim

Stolen by the Mountain Man

THE
IMPOSTER

ADRIANE LEIGH

Podium

Cover design by Claire Sullivan

ISBN: 979-8-3470-1640-2

Published in 2026 by Podium Publishing
www.podiumentertainment.com

THE IMPOSTER PLAYLIST

Love Will Probably Kill Me Before Cigarettes and Wine
Luke Spiller

Male Fantasy
Billie Eilish

Supercut
Lorde

Darling, I Want to Destroy You
AFI

King
Florence + The Machine

Real Life
The Marias

Fire
Black Pumas

Nothing's Gonna Hurt You Baby
Cigarettes After Sex

Kill Bill
SZA

The Weekend
Stormzy, RAYE

I Hate You, I Love You
Dr. Kid

Miss Murder
AFI

Fallen
Katastro

Tripping
The American Hotel System

VILLAIN
K/DA, Madison Beer, Kim Petras, League of Legends

Look What You Made Me Do
Taylor Swift

Guilty Conscience 2
Eminem

Paint The Town Red
Doja Cat

THE IMPOSTER

What is hell? Hell is oneself.
Hell is alone, the other figures in it
Merely projections. There is nothing to escape from
And nothing to escape to. One is always alone.

—T.S. Eliot

PROLOGUE

"Freedom isn't free." I smirk. "Isn't that what they say?"

Anger sizzles in his irises as he digests my words.

"This time, freedom will cost you a piece of yourself." My words linger in the air between us. "Maybe ten pieces." I toss the hammer at him, eyes twinkling.

"You're insane."

"Maybe, maybe not," I reply. "But do you really want to risk the chance that I'll have a change of heart?" I tease, enjoying this cat-and-mouse thing between us. "I can promise you, I won't."

CHAPTER 1

"Do you think your son resents you for divorcing his father?"

Mary sobs softly on my couch, then wipes her tears with a tissue. "I hope not. Gosh, that was years ago—"

"Kids have a way of holding onto the past. I know it sounds counterintuitive, but this is normal—he needs to kill you in his mind to find himself. It's just part of the process of parenthood, Mary. You know what I think you should do? I think you should spoil yourself with some self-care during this season of life."

Mary sniffs, and it takes everything in me not to roll my eyes. Mary's been talking to me for three sessions about how her teenage son wants nothing to do with her anymore. He's working, applying to colleges, spending time with his friends and a girlfriend, and Mary just can't get over that he doesn't have time for her in his life.

Every Monday at eleven, I find myself yawning through her session as she tearfully whines that she can't stop time.

I hate her. I do. But she pays my bills, so here I am, *enduring*.

"Self-care is a good idea. I've been walking the beach every evening before bed. That's been nice."

I nod, pretend to write something poignant in my notebook, and stifle another yawn. I don't know how Kelly sat there, day after day, listening to people complain about their lives. I thought this job would come with a little more . . . maybe not glamour, but *something*. The chance to be a fly on the wall of people's lives is far less interesting than I imagined. I find myself barely tolerating my patients most days. "Maybe add a morning walk to your routine or meet up with some friends for a coffee date?"

Mary considers my words, then composes herself. "You're always so thoughtful. Talking to you is the highlight of my week." She shifts on the couch. "You're an angel on earth."

I twirl the locket that reads *Kelly Bernice* hanging around my neck as I hum a soft "Thank you" and think that's what this has always been about—Mary pays me to be her friend, plain and simple. If only she knew the kind of friend I really am.

Mary stands and gathers her jacket and purse. "What was the name of that wellness resort you went to in the desert? With the cleanses and the yoga and sweat lodges?"

"Mm, yes. I'll get you the contact information for our next session. You would love it."

"I've been thinking maybe if I shed a few pounds and give myself a little reboot, it will improve my mood." Her eyes scan up and down my lean form. "You came back a different person, Doctor—twenty years younger, with that new hair too."

"You're sweet." I tuck my notebook into the side of my chair like Kelly always did after our sessions. I've lost sixty pounds in the four months since I walked out of Pacific View Psychiatric Hospital. There was no swanky wellness retreat and juice cleanse in the desert—there was only me, starving myself back to my original weight. Twenty-four-inch, pointy-straight blonde hair extensions and blood-red lipstick completed my transformation into the new Kelly Fraser, PhD. And throwing away that ratchet old Louis Vuitton bag Kelly carried was my first order of business.

Out with the old Louis, and in with the new is my new life motto.

"Well, I hope you have a good rest of your week." A warm, genuine smile crosses my lips. This is always my favorite part of the session—when it's over.

"Thank you, dear." Mary pats my arm and then excuses herself from my new home office. I stand at the open doorway and wave as she backs out of my driveway and then drives off down the street. I heave a sigh, ready to peel myself out of this professional sweater and pleated pant in favor of my bathing suit. Since the first day in my new rental cottage in Carmel Point—just outside of Carmel-by-the-Sea—I've been spencing every morning and evening at the beach. Kelly really spoiled herself when she prepaid for a lease on this charming beach cottage in a small gated community. With less than a dozen little cottages lining our private cul-de-sac, it's proven to be just the peaceful life I need after a decade of hell with Dean.

A cringe contorts my face at just the thought of him.

I'm ready to leave the past in the past. Kelly gave me a true gift when she failed to set the screen lock on her phone. I was able to take over her life—right down to her client bookings—without missing a beat. Kelly is the angel who helped me turn over a new leaf, and she doesn't even know it.

CHAPTER 2

"Ugh, could this be any tackier?" I half laugh as I pull out a colorful ceramic piece in the shape of a giant lollipop from a box of Kelly's things. She must've had movers pack everything up at her old place in LA and move it in ahead of her arrival. Digging through boxes of her shit has been revealing—the things she chose to bring with her as she stepped into this new life are telling at best and downright weird at worst.

First, I haven't found a single family memento. No photo albums, no childhood memories, not even so much as a family tree. When Kelly left her hometown in Arkansas for college, she really left. I smile, thinking how alike my former friend and I really are—running from the past straight into a future that isn't quite clear. I still find it funny that Kelly came all the way to Lake Tahoe for the weekend to spend time with me in my hour of need. She went above and beyond for me then, and I'm still trying to figure out *why*.

Surrounding myself with Kelly's things has helped me understand her better. It's an odd feeling, meeting with someone every week for twenty years and never really knowing them. Kelly made a fatal mistake thinking we were friends, but I realize now her desire for friendship was probably born out of loneliness. No children, no extended family, never any talk of friendships—she only ever had me. I was the constant in her life, as crazy as it sounds.

And I suppose she was the only constant in mine.

Do I miss her sometimes? Sure, on the days when I'm lost in my own head and can't seem to put one foot in front of the other, I often think to myself—*What would Kelly do?*

Conjuring her comforting smile always melts away the tension instantly. She has a special aura about her, a certain light that makes people open up and reveal things they wouldn't otherwise reveal to a stranger. It's special, but it's not something worthy of a degree that hangs on the wall in a shiny little diploma frame. I was born with the kind of charm Kelly has spent a lifetime cultivating in her therapy practice. I have a gift for people. So, in many ways, ending up right here feels like a natural progression. *God doesn't call the qualified. He qualifies the called,* I remember reading on an inspirational poster at the women's shelter in Tahoe. I used to believe my calling was to influence the masses with love and light and luxury living online, but now, it feels like my true purpose is right here, right now, in this moment. I was born for a time such as this—to impact real people on a meaningful level in a one-on-one setting—not just through sponsored brand posts on social media meant to reach the faceless thousands.

I tip my wineglass to my lips and empty its contents before setting the glass on the coffee table and standing from my cross-legged position on the floor. I gather the box of Kelly's worthless tchotchkes and carry it straight out the front door of my cottage to the garbage bin. With a grunt and a heave, I launch it into a bin. Dozens of ceramic pieces shatter in a satisfying cacophony as the box lands at the bottom of the trash. This is what I've had to do with most of Kelly's things. I should have known her taste was trash the way she hauled around that old Louis bag like it was her most prized possession.

I imagine her collecting the cheap ceramic pieces on vacations over her lifetime—always picking something "quirky" to commemorate the trip. But apparently no one ever taught Kelly that the line between tacky and trendy is razor-thin and she hasn't been walking it well. I grin as I saunter back into the house, thinking how liberating it feels to live like a minimalist. The ability to pick up and go at a moment's notice appeals to me. Where before my life revolved around superficial things like fashion and red-carpet events and white-tablecloth dinners, now I find a simple life at the beach and out of the spotlight agrees with me.

When I'm back in the cottage, I move to another stack of boxes labeled *Kitchen Decor*. I've been avoiding this stack of boxes—the last stack remaining—because throwing away things that Kelly thought were important enough to bring on her move from LA to Carmel isn't something I want on my conscience. But just like with that nasty old Louis bag, it's time to move on.

I gather the top moving box in my arms and return to the garbage bin, dumping the contents of the box into a can, so it makes a satisfying clatter of broken glass.

A sound not unlike the whistle of a boiling teapot reaches my ears. I turn to find a handsome man walking on the opposite side of the street with some sort of bulldog mix. Both the man's and the dog's eyes are on me before he says with a low chuckle, "Tell us how you really feel about that box."

Words catch in my throat, and the only thing I can think to do is give the man a quick wave. He smiles, then waves back before returning his attention to the dog and their walk. He doesn't turn around again, which is lucky for me, because if he did, he'd find me watching. I've never been much into overtly masculine, red-blooded men, but something about the way this man walks—an easy saunter that's both slow and light of foot, spine held straight, and a slight cock to his chiseled chin—has me captivated. I finally turn around and head back into the cottage when he's turned the corner of our cul-de-sac and is out of my sight.

"Well, that was a pleasant welcome to the neighborhood," I muse aloud as I return to the kitchen and open another bottle of pinot. I pour a full glass for myself before settling on the sofa and flipping on a TV series I've been watching that focuses on a therapist and his patients. I've been trying to soak up all the therapy lingo I can, even taking notes on some fictionalized cases that remind me of my own clients. It's been difficult trying to train my brain to think of them as *my* patients and not Kelly's, but if I have any chance of playing this role for the rest of my life, it's necessary.

The opening scene of the TV show starts, and I settle into the comfort of my new sofa. I've watched the entire first season so far, and my biggest takeaway is: Being a therapist is boring. No wonder Kelly lived such a bland life. She spent it soaking up other people's drama and never risking enough of anything to make her own. Kelly never needed a therapist because she was too fucking dull; I've come to realize what a bright star in her sky I must have been all those years. She was lucky to have Shae to add a little entertainment to her life among all the banal sob stories of anxiety and depression.

By the time the final scene of the episode is playing, I've taken some notes on new words in the therapy lexicon, along with a few thoughts on a strange case involving a woman who struggles to control her borderline personality. It feels like I've just sat in on a college lecture, and my brain is exhausted. It's been a lot of work familiarizing myself with Kelly's patients the last few months.

I move into my office, stopping a moment to take in a photo of Sophie and me that I keep on my desk. She's curled in my lap sucking her thumb, and a broad smile lights my face. She's still a toddler, and I'm about five. It's one of the few moments of pure joy captured in my childhood. Before the darkness descended. I push down a surge of emotion and lock the door of the office, then flip off the lights before making my way to the bathroom to get ready for bed.

As I brush my teeth, I think how easy it was to slide into Kelly's life as if I'd always been here. Kelly had already notified all her clients of her move. She had only one client scheduled in Carmel—Mary— and Mary was thankfully accommodating when I emailed to explain I was taking some much-needed time off to rest and recuperate after the move. Mary was sweet to allow me a few months to settle in. I took the time to brush up on my therapy skills, so when Mary and I had our first session, I flawlessly stepped into the role she expected. The only explanation I had to tackle was making her believe that my weight loss and visual transformation were all with the help of a little Botox, yoga, and juicing in the red rocks of Sedona.

Mary has been my testing ground. And now . . . now, I'm ready for more.

Within minutes, I'm settling into bed and curling up with the notebook I keep on the nightstand.

Shae Miller Halston is printed in thick black letters on the first page. I huff, thinking I'm not that girl anymore. I was never the girl Kelly thought I was—just like Mia Starr's followers, Kelly only knew the person I allowed her to see. I flip a few pages that detail my early diagnoses as a teenager—borderline personality and complex post-traumatic stress disorder, to name a few—and stop on a page from a session we had before Dean announced he wanted a divorce and upended my life. Kelly's scribbled shorthand reveals that she believed I was having dissociative episodes exacerbated by my online persona. Anger thickens my veins and runs through my body like slow-moving lava, gathering momentum with every passing diagnosis. I feel like Kelly's guinea pig, an experiment in clinical psychology for her own entertainment.

Did she realize that every time we spoke about *then*, I relived the trauma? I clamp my eyes closed in an attempt to shut out the memories.

"Girls!" my father calls through the house. His heavy bootsteps echo my thundering heartbeat. I cover my head with my pillow, pretending to sleep. His footfalls come closer, and I burrow deeper. "Girls!"

"Daddy!" Sophie squeals from beside me. She jumps on the bed, her tiny form bouncing with joy before he walks into our room and scoops her into his arms. I peek out from under the pillow, tears clouding my vision as I watch him swing her around and nuzzle into her neck. She's always been his favorite. I'm only older by three years, but those three years must be in dog years, because as soon as I was old enough to wash dishes, I did. As soon as I was old enough to fetch him beers while he watched the game, I did. And when I was tall enough to push his dirty laundry into the washing machine, I did that too.

"Daddy! Daddy! Dinner!" Sophie claps her hands.

"Are you hungry, baby girl?" She nods that she is. "Shae didn't make you something to eat? Shae, I told you to make your sister a peanut butter and jelly sandwich—"

"I didn't eat all day!"

"Shae, goddammit, I told you once your ma walked out on us, you'd have to pull your weight. We all do."

I throw the pillow off my head in a fit of rage. I think of my father's new girlfriend and how they've been insisting Sophie and I call her

Mom. In truth, I feel more like a parent to Sophie than the two of them combined. "But Sophie—"

"Sophie's practically a baby. It's not my fault your ma left. I have to work all day. Ain't got nobody to take care of your sister but you. Told you both not to fight and cry so goddamn much, then maybe she woulda stayed. Come on, baby girl." Sophie wiggles out of his arms and sneaks her hand into his. I move off the bed, but he holds up a hand to stop me. "Not you."

My eyes fall to his feet as he shuffles in the direction of the door. I notice him stumble, his hand holding tightly to Sophie's little fist as if her small form helps to keep him steady and grounded. He pauses when he reaches the door, catching my eyes and then directing his to the closet door. My heart sinks.

He must see the look of fear on my face because all he does is nod soundlessly.

I gulp, physical pain pulsing through me with each step I take. Tears burn my cheeks, but I try to be brave like my father always instructs. I don't like being brave, but I also don't want him to see me cry. It feels like crying is all I do since Mom left. And it feels like getting drunk and fighting with me is all Dad does now. I seem to be his replacement punching bag since Mom decided a life with us wasn't for her. Sophie is the only one who laughs anymore, and every time she does, I want to yell at her to shut up. Anything that takes his attention away from the TV or his drinking is a risk. One wrong look could land us here . . . in the closet.

I hiccup as I curl myself into the dark corner, but the soft snick of Dad closing and locking the door behind me causes a wave of comfort to wash over me. He's been locking us in this closet since she left, using the dark, confined space like a babysitter when he goes to work, spends time at the bar, or even plays cards with his friends. Like this is my own little cave, I've cried myself to sleep in this dark corner for as long as I can remember. Just like taking a Xanax, as soon as I step into the darkness, my breathing slows and the tears begin to dry. Now, the darkness calls to me. Secluded from the chaos, with only my tears to comfort me. In the darkness, I am home.

Numbness bleeds through my veins, loosens my muscles, and relaxes my mind. I scan the next few pages in Kelly's notebook as I try to shake the feelings of emptiness and neglect that, for so long, I thought were normal. I never confessed to Kelly how much time I spent in that closet—more hours than I spent in bed sleeping, if I tallied them.

I flip deeper into the notebook and my own psyche from Kelly's point of view over the years. The phrase *dangerously narcissistic sociopath* jumps out at me at the top of one of the pages in the back of the notebook. The page is dated from more than five years ago—well before Dean and Jesika and my life as Mia Starr. I take my time to read the next few sentences. *Lacks feeling for living things* is another phrase that stands out to me in Kelly's messy hand. I sigh, annoyed that this woman has been labeling me as fucking nuts this entire time while acting like my nearest and dearest friend. Hell, she was practically family in my darkest moments. I close the notebook and toss it on the bed beside me.

Kelly's Little Book of Lies is what I'm coming to think of this notebook.

Poring over her assessments of me each week has been a glimpse behind the curtain, and it's solidified the idea in my mind that we can choose to be whoever we want to be. And conversely, people can perceive us however they choose. It's the ultimate freedom—being whoever you want at any given moment with any given person.

I still think of Kelly as a traitor who deserved what she got, but I can't deny that she's helped me see myself clearer. She's helped me discover who I am and who I am not. And who I am is *definitely* not the sad, broken girl in that notebook.

I'll make sure of it.

CHAPTER 3

"Do you think he really loves us?" Sophie singsongs as she adds another brushstroke of paint the color of flesh to her paper.

"I mean . . . what is love?" I say as I rinse a handful of spoons under the faucet until the soap suds vanish down the drain. "If keeping a roof over our heads is love, then sure." I wash a bunch of forks, rinse them, then drop them on the kitchen towel to dry. "If love means a safe place to sleep with three square meals a day and warm hugs from someone who doesn't call you a failure? Then maybe not so much." I wash and rinse a palmful of steak knives.

"He doesn't say that kind of stuff to me," Sophie muses. "I feel love from him, I think. Not often, and I know he forgets dinner a lot, but skipping a meal now and again won't kill us."

I grip the steak knives so tightly in my hand, the jagged teeth cut into my palm. Tiny pinpricks of blood appear, but I rinse them away under the stream of cool water.

"He feeds you more than he feeds me," I state. She knows this. We've talked about this before. She is his favorite. He's made that clear plenty of times.

"I try to bring food up to you on those nights," Sophie says, almost defensively. I guess I would feel shame too if I was eating cheeseburgers

and fries while my sister was locked in a closet upstairs without dinner. "You shouldn't talk back to him, Shae. You just have to be nice, and he'll like you."

"That's not how it's supposed to be. I shouldn't have to beg him to like me. I shouldn't have to earn his love."

"It's just for a little while." Sophie's voice is weak. Every time she laughs, I want to stab something. How is she so easy to be around, while I live with a monster on my shoulder, waiting for the other shoe to drop?

"I hope he stops at Joe's after work," I say, thinking of my father sitting at his favorite barstool in his favorite bar. Sophie and I practically grew up at Joe's. Half of our family meals over the years were hot dogs and french fries while Dad played darts and guzzled cans of Budweiser. "Then maybe he'll come home and pass out on the couch, and we'll have a peaceful night."

"But if he stops at the bar, he might not come home alone." Sophie's words are calm but laced with pain. It was weird waking up to strange women in the house when we were little kids, but now at six and nine— old enough to know what they're doing behind closed doors—it's downright disgusting. Even more so when he lets them stay the night, and they crawl out of bed and walk around the house in his old shirts, smelling like him.

So far, it seems like Sophie has mostly escaped the abuses of my father, his gloating praise for her always at the ready. In contrast, he wears his disdain for me on his sleeve. Sophie is quiet and poised, the same expressive dark eyes and fine features as my mother. At least, what I can remember of her, anyway. Dad threw every photo we had of her into the fire pit one hot summer night. The last time I laid eyes on my mother's face, fire licked at the edges of her blonde curls before she evaporated into smoke. If setting her likeness on fire was meant to cleanse him of his pain, it hasn't worked.

Every year since, his alcoholism has seemed to outdo itself; his rages last longer and come more frequently. I spend more time in the closet, not because he locks me in anymore, but because it is the only place to escape him. Fear has drilled holes so deeply into my mind that any strange noise at night jerks me out of my restless sleep. I am always terrified he's coming for me.

While Sophie escapes into her imagination, painting pictures that win class art shows, I've retreated into myself. Now, my killer comes from within—assaulting me with the same stones and arrows he's been hurling at me since I could talk. And just like him, my dark obsessions have grown with time too.

When my dad rages, I imagine he'll hurt Sophie. Just once, I wish she would be the outlet for his anger, his palms around her neck choking off her air while he berates her for acting like a baby. But Sophie is too polite, too naive, too patient with his pain. She pretends she understands him, while I just don't care. I've found that once my anger bubbles to the surface, stopping it becomes impossible.

"Sophie, what a masterpiece." Dad's voice bellows through the kitchen. I can tell by his quick, clipped tone that he is sober. But he won't be for long. "Let me see it better." He plants a palm on her shoulder. A look of pride flickers in his eyes as they roam the half-finished painting. "What an artist—my sensitive little bird." He drops a kiss on her head, squeezes her shoulder, and then pulls away. "Was telling the guys at work just today how proud I am of my little girl—so much talent. You must get it from your old dad." He grins down at her. Her dark eyes sparkle to life under his praise. No wonder she doesn't hate him. He loves her.

Hatred thickens in my veins as he walks out of the kitchen without so much as a glance my way. Sophie bends, dips the tip of her brush in more paint, and then works on a dandelion in the lower-right corner of the paper.

I clutch a steak knife in my trembling hand; the desire to see it plunged into my father's throat is almost overwhelming. I imagine his blood painting the paper, and a smile comes to my face. My hatred is so pure, I can taste it. I don't know if pure love exists, but I know pure hate does. I know because the surge of warmth it sends through me is intoxicating.

I'm thinking of killing him, *I write in my tiny journal a while later. I only write my darkest thoughts in the small journal with the lock. I carry the key around with me everywhere because I know Dad would flay me alive if he knew what I was actually thinking. I finger the locket I found in Mom's jewelry drawer after she left. Inside is nestled a picture of Sophie and me, our chubby cheeks grinning widely.* The years I don't remember are the happiest of my life, *I write.* I've been wondering a lot lately what life would be like without Sophie. Then would Dad have enough room in his heart for me? Would his stress be less if there was one less mouth to feed? Maybe Sophie's demanding cries keep him in a constant state of agitation. The desire to protect her from his wrath is strong. Maybe this is one more thing I can take care of for us. Maybe taking action would simplify our lives.* I want to go to college, but how can I when they need me all the time? *I write.* I just want freedom. I just want escape. But how can I when I feel chained to this family just like my mother?

I've often thought that if Sophie hadn't been born, maybe our mom wouldn't have left. Maybe the stress of having two babies drove her away. I am the one so attuned to my father's needs that he would be lost without me. Sophie doesn't know how to cook or clean or do laundry. She's so innocent and naive, one stern look from my father and she bursts into inconsolable tears. Maybe that's why she escaped his terror. Maybe I should have cried more. But I don't have tears inside me. There is nothing. Only a black hole exists where my emotions should live. When

Sophie bursts into tears, my anger sizzles and pops like damp wood in a campfire.

I think of the rat poison Dad keeps under the kitchen sink and wonder how much it would take to stop his beating heart. I can't take all of his swinging emotions on top of taking care of Sophie and her constant bleeding heart. All I can think is, what does she have to cry about when I'm the one taking care of all of us? What would happen if I broke down and hid in bed all day? I would be locked in the closet, that's what.

My mind drifts to the prescription medication I found in the bathroom vanity. I don't know what it's used for—only that every time my father uses it, he passes out on the couch, practically dead, all night long. It's the most peace we ever get, so I swiped a few pills for myself. I considered taking one just to see what would happen, but my fear of the unknown is strong. Instead, crushing half a pill to put in Sophie's apple juice feels like the better course of action to keep her calm while I kill him. I'm exhausted from trying so hard to protect them from each other, maybe even themselves. I don't know what half a pill will do to my six-year-old sister, but I know one thing—this life is killing me. I can't help but wonder if it would be better to cease to exist than live in abuse? *I scribble in my journal. My father's heavy footsteps fall on the stairs then, and I slam my journal closed and shove the key in the lock quickly. I push the journal under my pillow just as he swings open the door to our room.*

"Where's Sophie?" he bellows.

"She fell asleep in the closet," I spit.

"Don't talk to me that way." Dad hauls me off the bed. His grip on my elbow is painful. I know I'll have bruises in the shape of his fingertips in the morning. It's fitting that he leaves marks on my body. I like it because it's a visual representation that the pain inside me is real. Without the reminder, it's easy to slip inside myself, imagine I'm making

up the pain that has burrowed deep in my heart. After all, is emotional pain even real pain at all? While these future bruises hurt, they're no comparison to the pain of my broken heart.

"I need this place spotless. Got a friend coming over tonight. Clean, make Sophie some dinner, then spend the rest of the night in your room, got it?" he barks as he pulls me down the stairs with him. "Don't need you two runnin' off another woman in my life."

CHAPTER 4

"Shit!" I spit toothpaste into the sink as the doorbell rings another time. "Coming!"

I straighten my blazer in the mirror and then speed down the short hallway and through the sitting room to the office at the front corner of the house. Kelly must have chosen this cottage because of the private entrance off this front room; she can see patients without ever letting them into her home space.

When I open the door for my first brand-new patients in Carmel, my mouth drops.

"Hi," is all I can think to say.

"Mornin'." The thirst trap with the dog from yesterday is standing on my doorstep with a charming smile. "I'm Isaac Rawlins."

"And I'm Brianna." I finally notice the petite woman standing at his side.

I nod, words still lodged in my throat. I'm captivated by this man's eyes, a bright shade of peridot rimmed with flecks of gold.

Isaac clears his throat. "We have an appointment for marriage counseling."

"Oh, of course," I murmur, moving aside so they can come into my office.

"Welcome to the neighborhood. I'm sorry we didn't stop by before now. It's been a busy season for us. Isaac's been traveling for work, and my schedule has been all over the place. It's so exciting to have a therapist in the neighborhood. We've been here since we got married, and all we usually get for neighbors is a revolving door of retirees. I figured, therapy and a new friend to drink wine and watch *The Bachelor* with—two birds with one stone!" She finally stops speaking. "Do you watch *The Bachelor*?"

Her wide-eyed innocence grates on me for reasons I can't quite name.

"Sure," I finally answer. "I catch it now and again. I'm not caught up though."

"Well, we'll hafta change that." Her smile is wide and toothy, and I can't help but wonder if she's always this open with complete strangers. "You do like wine, right? I mean, who moves to wine country and doesn't like wine?"

"I do," I reply. She nods, eyes finally cutting from mine to the floor under my feet. "Well, it's nice to meet you. I think I saw you yesterday walking your dog . . ."

Isaac's lips turn into a devastating, crooked grin. "I was going to walk him down here with us, but I wasn't sure if you were a dog person or not."

Well, Isaac is clearly a dog person, and henceforth, so am I. "I love them." I smile, holding his eyes. "Please, bring him next time. I think dogs are the perfect therapy companion, so soothing for the central nervous system."

Brianna nods, eyes big and warm as she takes me in. "What made you move to Carmel Point?"

"Have a seat on the sofa." I gesture them into my office and then close the door behind them. "I've been in LA for the last two decades. I just needed a change of scenery."

"It's definitely a slower pace up here. That's why we love it too." Brianna hooks her arm with her husband's as she sits on the sofa beside him. "Isaac's from the area—Santa Cruz—and I'm—"

My vision tunnels with her words. I can't hear anything else she's saying, because it's then I realize why Isaac is so familiar.

I know him.

I struggle to sit across from them now, the perfect picture of empathy, nodding as they recount their grievances. *Brianna and Isaac.* Brianna is talking about how distant Isaac has become, how he spends more time at work than with her. Isaac's eyes are downcast, his guilt evident. I sip my tea, savoring the bitterness, letting it linger on my tongue.

"It's important to create a space where both of you feel heard," I finally say, my voice smooth and comforting. "Isaac, why don't you tell Brianna what you're feeling?"

Isaac shifts in his seat, hesitant. "I . . . I feel overwhelmed at work. I don't want to burden Brianna with it."

I lean forward, my eyes locking onto Brianna's. "And how does that make you feel, Brianna?"

She sighs, tears welling up. "It makes me feel like I'm not important to him."

Perfect. I reach out, placing a hand on hers. "Brianna, your feelings are valid. Isaac, it's crucial that Brianna feels valued in this relationship."

Isaac nods, his face a mask of contrition. I smile inwardly. This is too easy.

"Have you considered spending more quality time together? Maybe a weekend getaway?" I suggest. Isaac's eyes widen slightly, a flicker of panic. Good.

"That's a great idea," Brianna says, her voice hopeful. "Isaac, what do you think?"

Isaac hesitates but nods. "Yes, we can do that."

I sit back, satisfied. My plan is working perfectly. Brianna is growing more dependent on my guidance, and Isaac is being pushed further into a corner. They won't last much longer if I have my way.

I glance at the clock, it's hardly been forty-five minutes since they walked in my door, but I can't sit here listening to them any longer. "Our time is almost up for today. Let's reconvene next week and see how things are progressing. Remember, communication is key."

They stand, thanking me as they leave. I watch them go, a smile playing on my lips. Just a little more time, and I'll have them exactly where I want them.

CHAPTER 5

Does he remember me?

This question runs on a constant loop in my mind as I punch the letters of Isaac's name into my laptop keyboard an hour later. I can still smell the crisp ocean scent of his cologne lingering in my office as his name comes up instantly in my search results. In another moment, I've located all his social media profiles. I know it's him because his gorgeous, lopsided smile is peering back at me from all of the photos. Some seem to have been taken in a work environment—the waves of golden blond he wears now, which make him look like a California surfer boy, are gone in favor of a slicked-back businessman style that makes him almost unrecognizable. In other photos, he's playing with his dog or attending family events—his distinct lopsided grin and peridot eyes always immediately identifiable.

Warm tingles swallow me as I realize he looks exactly the same as I remember him from high school. I haven't thought of him in nearly two decades . . . not since *that* night.

I realize then that two men were present during the most destructive moments of my life—Dean and this man. Isaac knew me before I was Mia or Kelly. He knew Shae before tragedy spoiled my life like rotten fruit.

Isaac was the first man I ever loved. He was also the first man I ever wanted to kill.

Flashbacks that haven't seen the light of day in decades flit through my consciousness. I buried everything about the summer I met Isaac Rawlins—and for good reason. That man left me with bags of trauma I still haven't unpacked. In fact, I'm pretty sure I buried everything about Isaac in the deepest reaches of my mind until now. Until he sauntered by my house like a ghost from a past life.

I blink away a memory of Isaac in his high school letterman's jacket. Isaac being crowned homecoming king before clinching the win against a rival football team as the star running back. Everyone knew Isaac Rawlins; Isaac made sure of it. And while most people peak in high school, Isaac only seems to have become more driven. I find his business page on LinkedIn—he's been an entrepreneur since he graduated with a business degree from a private college outside of Santa Cruz, where he played football all four years. A lightning strike of pain pierces my heart as another memory about that summer night comes back to me. I blink away fresh tears that I've been doing my best not to feel for two decades. I breathe deeply as I think about what Kelly would tell me to do. We worked so hard to undo the damage that night caused, but some days, the wound feels like it still festers just under the surface. It's on those days it takes everything in me to distract myself.

Another errant memory trickles through my mind, and I blink it away, suck in a breath, and then slam my laptop closed and stand. It's not healthy for me to fixate like this—especially online. I already know too much about him. I've already crossed some sort of line that I don't think Kelly ever crossed with me, when she so easily could have. Did she ever look up Mia Starr, my online influencer persona, after one of our sessions? If she did, she never let on. I'll have to do my best to forget what I know about Isaac during his sessions.

I linger for a moment at the doorway of the cottage before deciding a quick walk to the beach is just the distraction I need. It takes me two minutes to change into my new bathing suit and cover-up and slip on my old sneakers. I take my time as I walk along the quiet, begonia-lined street down to the end of the cul-de-sac. I'm acutely aware that one of these little cottages belongs to Isaac and Brianna. It's surprising I haven't run into them before now, but then, I've been keeping to myself these last few months as I find myself in Kelly's life. I casually scan the charming, picket-fenced front yards of the cottages at this corner of the street, looking for any clue that might indicate which is theirs. Nothing stands out, so I turn onto the wooded pathway that meanders down the side of a hill before ending at the beach.

I slip off my sneakers and spend the next twenty minutes walking through the surf. The water is cleansing for my soul, and I think not for the first time how grateful I am that Kelly was called to this place. She would have loved it, I'm sure of it. There's even a glimmer of guilt that descends as I think about where she is now. I don't have any idea where she's being kept, and I haven't bothered to look. If I'm to really, authentically become Kelly, I have to kill her once and for all. Anyway, she's worked so hard for so long, given so much in service of her career. But for what? To live alone with all her meaningless knickknacks? I gave her an extended sabbatical. She'll have all the rest and relaxation she can get now.

Anyway, if I've learned anything over the last few months of becoming Kelly, I'm a better her anyway.

I turn to head back to my cottage and get ready for my afternoon video session with a new client, when I see him. He's just coming down the wooded pathway that leads to our cul-de-sac, chubby dog at the end of his leash. I dig my toes into the sand as I watch him come closer. Isaac bends, unhooks the dog from his leash, and lets him pick his way along rocks and driftwood at the base of the hill. My heart rattles wildly as I consider what to do next. If I continue home, I can't avoid him.

I shake my head then, thinking how silly I'm being. I have a client, I have things to do, I can't take the long way home just to avoid this man who may or may not remember me. I groan softly when he peels his T-shirt over his head—he's built like a marble Greek god. Tall and lean, he has defined and broad shoulders, while his waist is cut narrowly. He bends, spends a few moments stretching, and then drops to the sand and does a dozen push-ups. It takes everything in me not to spontaneously combust. He's even more handsome than he was in high school—more muscled and defined—and the intense cut of his jawline and unruly waves of slightly too-long hair give him both a grown man and a boyish quality that I've never seen in someone before.

Where Dean is serious and fatherly, Isaac is charming and playful.

I ache then for the kind of romantic love that makes me feel lighthearted, not constantly criticized and scrutinized. Awareness hums to life as I flash back to another night when Isaac walked me home from my job at the ice cream parlor. We were sixteen, and with his hand wrapped around mine, I remember feeling safe and loved and cared for—protected and wanted and desired and so special. I can't imagine I left the same impact on him that he did on me. Isaac Rawlins is the kind of guy that leaves an impression. In truth, our time together wasn't anything more than a summer fling, a few hot weeks before we went our separate ways.

I suck in a measured breath and walk in slow strides in the direction of the man who represents everything I hate about my past. He was the one shining star in my dark sky. Until he *wasn't*. Until he spoiled everything and vanished from my life as quickly as he'd come into it.

As I draw nearer, Isaac's gaze finally meets mine. One corner of his mouth lifts in that handsome crooked grin, and he gives me a friendly wave.

"Hi," I say as I approach. "Should I be worried I have a stalker?" I tease.

Isaac chuckles, and his eyes sparkle when he does. "Two, in fact." His dog finds me at that moment, and with his tail wagging furiously, he dips in between my legs and circles me excitedly in search of attention. I giggle and bend, scratching behind his ears as he attacks me with puppy kisses. "Dr. Fraser, meet King Louie."

It takes me a moment to register that he's just called me by a name I'm not used to. "Please, just Kelly."

He nods and bends, picking up a piece of driftwood and throwing it as far as he can. The dog chases after it, but instead of bringing it back, he lies down and starts chewing the stick. Isaac shrugs and sends me another quick smile.

I sink my top teeth into my bottom lip. He's captivating—the all-star, prom king playboy, all grown-up and domesticated. I can't help but love the idea of wresting him away from his real life and reminding him what fun we used to have. That roguish grin and mischievous twinkle are all the indication I need that the fun side of him is buried just beneath a layer of responsibility and obligation. I am the master of the pivot—Dean and Jesika and Bishop and Kelly, heck, even my followers when I worked as Mia Starr prove that—but can I really pivot this man away from his life and into my hands?

I let a shy smile fall onto my lips as I look up at him, my head lowered. "I was thinking . . . it might be more productive if you and your wife have separate counseling sessions going forward."

His eyebrows lift with surprise before he replies, "Sure, Doc. Whatever you think is best."

CHAPTER 6

"Okay, girls. Listen up. We don't have much time." My father's sky-blue eyes are bloodshot and hazy in the rearview mirror. "You know how I said I ain't takin' care of the lawn at the golf course anymore?"

Both of us nod. Dad explained last week he lost his landscaping contract, so we were out of money. We got by on what was left in the pantry, while Dad drank whiskey all day long "to forget," he said. But the food ran out last night, and Sophie's been complaining all day that her tummy hurts. I finally convinced him to drive us to the food mart across town. He'd stopped for the bottle of whiskey on the way here. I wonder if his whiskey cost more than the sandwiches we're about to steal for dinner.

"You girls have to earn your meals. Told ya everyone's got to grow up sometime." He grins, and the tooth behind his canine is missing. He looks like a villain in one of Sophie's favorite cartoons. I hate him so much that sometimes I vibrate with anger while Sophie sleeps peacefully at my side in our old twin bed. "This'll make you street-smart, anyway, and that's a helluva lot better than anything you're gonna learn in those schoolbooks." He pulls on the bottle, burps, then twists the cap back on. "Don't teach ya what really happened, anyway. It's all bullshit. Don't listen to 'em."

We don't say anything, probably because we're not really sure who "them" is.

"Goddamn golf club prick hirin' a new landscaper. I checked 'em out. The golf club is their only client. Biggest goddamn employer in town, and I've had their contract for two fucking decades. But when your nephew starts a new landscapin' business, I guess you go ahead and hire him. So much for loyalty. Tell you what, girls. You can't trust any of them rich assholes. They're all the fucking same. Profit over people. Losin' that contract is gonna put us out on the street, while that family wallows like fat pigs in a pile of money and shit. Don't depend on nobody but yourself—that's why it's good you're learnin' how to feed yourselves now. Life skills are important. And anyway, ain't nobody gonna think twice if you tuck a few sandwiches in the pockets of your jackets, okay?"

Sophie's eyes hang on my father's every movement. He turns into a parking spot at the mega mart, then slides the gear shift into park and turns to look at us.

"You got big pockets in that jacket, Shae. You think you can fit an extra sandwich in there for dear old dad?"

Sophie giggles like he's just said the funniest thing. She's only seven; I guess everything is funny at that age. I was only there a few years ago, but seven for me looked a lot different than for Sophie. Dad twists the top off his whiskey bottle and then takes another long pull from it.

"Sure, Dad," I croak as I open the back door.

Dad catches my eye in the rearview. "Make it quick."

"I always do," I say under my breath.

My hands feel icy as we walk across the parking lot, like I've been holding them out in the cold too long, but it's just the nerves tingling through me. Sophie clutches at my sleeve, her small fingers twisted in the fabric as we stand at the entrance of the local market. Her big, trusting eyes look up at me, waiting for instruction.

"Remember, Soph, we have to be quick and quiet. No one should notice us, okay?" I whisper, scanning the store layout I've memorized over countless other trips.

Sophie nods, her face set in a determined frown. It's a look I taught her, one that's necessary for moments like this. Dad's waiting in the car, counting on us. He says no one suspects little kids, and even if they do, what are they gonna do? Arrest us? The thought makes my stomach twist, not with fear, but anger. Why is this our life?

I take Sophie's hand, squeezing it reassuringly as we slip between the aisles. The market buzzes with the regular noise of carts rolling and cash registers beeping, a comforting hum under which we can become invisible. My eyes dart around, watching the workers as they stock shelves and help customers. When I'm sure none of them are looking our way, I steer Sophie toward the deli section.

The sandwiches are lined up neatly, wrapped in clear plastic that reflects the harsh overhead lights. My heart beats faster, and I can feel Sophie's hand tremble in mine. "Just the sandwiches," I remind her, seeing her eyes linger on the candy aisle.

I grab three sandwiches—turkey and cheese, simple and not too fancy. They don't draw much attention. I slide two into my jacket pockets and the third into the big pocket on the front of Sophie's faded overalls. She knows better than to move too much now, holding herself still, her small body rigid with the weight of our theft.

As we turn to leave, I feel the weight of every step, each one heavier than the last as we move toward the exit. Just before we can make our escape, Mrs. Dalton, a cashier who's known Dad since before his drinking got bad, stops us.

"Hello, Shae, Sophie." She greets us with a warm smile that reaches her eyes. "How's your father?"

I force a smile, my cheeks stiff. "He's okay, thanks. Just busy with work."

Sophie beams up at her, innocent and unaware of the irony in my words. Mrs. Dalton nods, her gaze flickering down to Sophie, then back to my face. There's a knowing there, a silent acknowledgment that maybe she sees more than she lets on.

"Take care, girls," she says, her voice soft, almost too kind. It makes guilt gnaw at me, a feeling I despise more than hunger.

"Thank you, Mrs. Dalton," I reply, pulling Sophie gently by the hand to finally step out into the cool evening air.

The walk to the car is silent except for the crunch of gravel under our sneakers. Dad's old sedan is parked at the far end of the lot, away from prying eyes. He's slumped in the driver's seat, a cigarette dangling from his lips. His eyes light up when he sees us—a look reserved only for moments when we bring food.

"Did you get them?" he asks, the car filled with the smell of smoke and spilled whiskey.

Sophie, ever the eager child, nods enthusiastically and hands him the sandwich from her pocket. "We got dinner, Daddy!"

He chuckles, ruffling her hair. "Good girls. We'll try the market on Fifth tomorrow. Can't go to the same place too often."

I slide into the passenger seat, my hands finally warming up, but the cold inside me doesn't fade. I stare out the window, the neon lights of the market sign blurring as we drive away. I was so hungry all day, imagining biting into one of those sandwiches. But now, with the taste of shame lingering on my tongue, I can't imagine eating.

Sophie munches on her sandwich in the back seat, her small voice humming a tuneless song of contentment. She's happy just to be fed, blissfully unaware of the cost. But I know. I know all too well.

Dad glances over at me, his eyes narrowing. "Aren't you eating, Shae?"

I shake my head, my voice barely a whisper. "Not hungry."

He shrugs, turning his attention back to the road. The silence settles back around us, heavy and thick.

As the car hums beneath me, I close my eyes and try to imagine a different life, where stealing isn't our normal, where Dad looks at me with pride instead of expectation. I have to believe in karma—that somehow, someway, there's a balance to all this. That belief is all I have left—it's what keeps me from shattering completely. It has to be enough. It just has to be.

CHAPTER 7

I purse my lips in the mirror once, then apply a thick layer of my favorite red lipstick. Flipping my hair a few times, I give it some volume with a quick spray of dry shampoo and then adjust my cleavage in the mirror.

Isaac will be here any minute.

It's been a few days since we talked on the beach. A few days since I managed to convince him that private sessions would be more beneficial than joint sessions with him and Brianna. It wasn't even hard. If I'm reading him right, I would even say he's looking for just the kind of fun I have in mind.

The doorbell buzzes and shakes me out of my thoughts. It's go time. I leave the bathroom and cross the hallway in quick steps, then swing the door open with a warm smile. Isaac's staring back at me, and the dog wags his tail as he peers up at me.

"Hey, guys!" I affect a bubblier tone than is natural for me. I wouldn't say I'm being fake—Isaac does make me feel giggly like a schoolgirl—but I'm looking to leave him with the impression that I am easy and carefree. I'm trying to reflect the same don't-give-a-care surfer-boy attitude he seems to manifest so naturally.

"Hope we're not too early." He smiles easily, and then, for just a moment, I see his gaze flick down to my cleavage. My grin deepens as I realize I have him. He's the same red-blooded male he always was, and that's something I can work with. That's an energy I know how to use in my favor and manipulate for my own amusement. If he was happily married, he wouldn't have a wandering eye. In fact, the sooner I can expose this man to his wife and take him off her hands, the better off she'll be.

He might be her problem right now, but I'll give anything to make him mine. Isaac Rawlins is just the kind of project I like.

"You're right on time." I open the door and stand aside to let him and his dog inside. The dog sniffs his way around my small office and then climbs up on the sofa and sits, looking up at us expectantly.

"Off the sofa. Come on, you know better." Isaac waves at the dog, but he just continues to sit there.

"He's fine. I don't mind," I say helpfully.

"Guess I shoulda brought some treats. He always gets a treat after his walk." Isaac scratches him behind his ear. "That's what you're waitin' for, huh, boy?"

"I might have something . . ." I don't. I know I don't, but I want to offer just the same.

"It's all right. He likes cuddles almost as much." Isaac sits down on the sofa next to his dog. The fat dog inches across the cushion until he's almost fully leaning against Isaac's hard body. I'd give anything to be that dog right now, and in time, I will. I know it. Good things don't happen overnight. I'll wait patiently, like a snake in the grass waiting for just the right moment to strike.

I settle opposite Isaac in my chair and cross my legs. My already-short skirt inches a little higher up my thigh. A thrill of excitement courses through me when I see his gorgeous golden-green gaze slide up my legs quickly until they pause at my cleavage and then flutter closed a moment as a grin lifts a corner of his lips. All I can think about is closing the distance between us and sliding into his lap to latch onto his full lips, but not yet. Not yet.

"So, tell me about Brianna." I open the notebook I've designated just for Isaac.

He clears his throat and begins. "We started dating in high school and got married the same year I graduated college. We've been together for . . . a long time. I know her better than myself, and I used to think that was a good thing. But I'm not so sure anymore. I agree with you about individual sessions being better for us. She kept insisting on marriage counseling, but as far as I'm concerned, we communicate *too* damn much. When I'm not traveling for work, I'm home all day long. We communicate constantly. All she does is tell me about how she feels."

"And how does she feel?" I scratch Brianna's name in the notepad and circle it a few times.

"Unfulfilled. Bored. I don't know. However wives feel after over a decade of marriage."

I raise my eyebrows. His openness is refreshing. Most men are so tight-lipped, they find anything more than football or the weather an uncomfortable conversation.

"You've been together for a long time." I state the obvious.

He just nods. "We were too young. Seems silly now to believe that the person you meet at fourteen will be the same person you're compatible with at thirty-four."

I scribble Isaac's name in the notebook with a few stars and hearts surrounding it. "Some people grow together, and some grow apart."

He hums, and when I look up from my notebook, I find his gaze hanging heavy on mine. "There's something about you . . ."

My eyebrows shoot up my forehead before I catch my reaction and smile. "I'm not sure why."

He squints, tips his head to the side, crooked grin deepening. My heart catches when he does this. It's exactly the same look he used to give me right before his hands slipped down my pants and our lips connected in a passionate kiss back then. This dual side to him, the way he's so carefree and playful with most people and then intensely charming and sensual when he's turned on, bewitched me then and still does.

His voice lowers an octave. "Are you from here, Doc?"

My heart skips a beat when I answer. "I've never been here before."

One eyebrow rises as if he doesn't believe me. "How long have you had a private practice?"

What is this, a police interview? "Most days, I think too long."

His lips crack into a wide grin. "I hear that." He scratches his dog behind the ear and then murmurs, "Sometimes I think that's part of the problem. We didn't know ourselves when we said *I do* . . . Well, maybe she did, but I sure as hell didn't. And I gave so much of myself to her, to us. My parents have such a solid marriage—thirty-five years in and I still see them making time for each other and nurturing their relationship. But . . . I just . . . I've just been nurturing *us* for so long, I think I missed out on some other important life steps."

"Oh?" I try to suppress a knowing smile.

"I invested so much into her when I probably should have invested more time, energy, and money into starting my business. I feel like I've spent all of my marriage fighting my natural impulses, just to make her happy."

"Your natural impulses?" I inquire innocently.

He huffs. "I have two failed businesses under my belt since I earned my business degree, and a third is about to be flushed down the toilet. And all Brianna can think about is us having enough time and money to start a family and still maintain our emotional connection and make sure we can afford spring in Cabo and Christmas in Aspen . . . It's just . . . she comes from a world with a lot of expectation attached, and really . . . I don't give a fuck anymore."

I don't say anything, waiting to see if he'll reveal more. Already, he's exposed his weakness—it's just like I imagined—the all-star homecoming king all grown up has a wicked fear of missing out on life. This man lives for adventure, competition, the hunt. He's a wild animal that was never meant to be caged. And now, it's up to me to lead him back to the wilderness where he belongs.

With me.

And Isaac, bless his heart, is making it so easy.

CHAPTER 8

The wind picks up as we walk along the coastline, the sunset casting long, golden shadows across the path. Isaac reaches for my hand, his touch warm and surprisingly calming. I can hardly believe this is real—that Isaac, the star running back and undisputed heartthrob of Santa Cruz High, wants to hold my hand. His fingers lace through mine with an ease that sends shivers up my arm, not from the evening chill, but from the sheer excitement of his nearness.

"So, this is nice, huh?" Isaac says, his voice smooth and comforting against the rush of the waves at our feet. I nod, my words catching in my throat.

"It's beautiful," I manage to say, feeling a bit cliché but truthful nonetheless.

Isaac stops, turning to face me, his eyes searching mine. "Not as beautiful as you, Shae," he says, and it's so earnest, so sincere, that for a moment I forget to breathe.

I laugh, a nervous, disbelieving sound. "Come on, Isaac. You don't have to say things like that."

He smiles, that heart-stopping grin that I've seen light up count-less hallways and classrooms. "But I mean it," he insists. "I've always noticed you, you know? There's something about you—your spirit, your wit. It's . . . real. And beautiful."

I feel a blush creep up my cheeks, burning hotter than the setting sun. No one has ever spoken to me like this, especially not someone like Isaac, who could have any girl he wants. Why would he choose me, with my second-hand clothes and my life that's anything but perfect?

"You don't have to try so hard to make me feel good," I say, looking down at our intertwined fingers.

Isaac lifts my chin gently, so I'm looking into his eyes again. "Shae, I'm not saying it just to make you feel good. I'm saying it because it's true. I broke up with Brianna because I'm tired of the games, the drama. I want something real, and I think I found that with you."

I want to believe him, more than anything, but doubts cloud my mind like the shadows that creep across the path as the sun sinks lower. Brianna and her gang of friends have made it clear what they think of me. I've heard the taunts, felt the sting of their words. "But Brianna is . . . she's everything I'm not," I say, the words heavy with the weight of my insecurities.

Isaac shakes his head, his expression serious. "Brianna is mean, Shae. She's spoiled. I'm sick of being around someone who makes other people feel small just to build herself up. You're nothing like her, and that's a good thing. You're kind, you're funny, and you're strong, so much stronger than you think."

His words wash over me like the waves beside us, strong and steady and sure. It's hard to hold onto my doubts when he looks at me like I'm the only person in the world.

"Look, I know it's hard to believe sometimes, especially with everything you've been through," he continues, squeezing my hand. "But I like you, Shae. I like you a lot. And I'm here because I want to be here, with you."

The sincerity in his voice chips away at the walls I've built around my heart. Maybe, just maybe, he means what he says. Maybe Isaac isn't like the others who've hurt me—my absent mom, my drunk dad, Brianna and her gang of mean girls who mock me so cruelly. It feels like everyone in my life has decided I wasn't worth their time. Until now. Until Isaac.

"So, what do you say, Shae? Will you let me prove it to you? Let me be the one to make you smile?" His eyes are hopeful, and in them, I see a future I never dared to imagine.

A future where I'm not defined by my past, by my hardships, or by the cruel words of someone like Brianna. A future where someone like Isaac could really like me for who I am.

"Okay," I whisper, and it feels like the biggest leap of faith I've ever taken. But as he smiles and pulls me closer, wrapping his arm around my shoulders as we resume walking, I feel a spark of hope flicker to life inside me.

"Wanna go back to my house?" His words are laced with innuendo. My stomach flips. I've never been with a man before. Isaac is my first boyfriend, my first kiss, my first everything.

"Okay," I breathe, trying to control the nerves vibrating in my veins. Isaac leads me in the direction of his car, his palm locked with mine as we walk.

Maybe there is happiness in my future after all. And maybe, just this once, I'll allow myself to believe that it's possible. With Isaac, I have hope. And maybe that's enough to start rewriting my story.

CHAPTER 9

"Hmm . . . a beach wedding. How sweet." I flip past another photo of Isaac's and Brianna's smiling faces. Bath bubbles surround me as I soak in the tub and scroll through Isaac's family's social media feeds. While Isaac keeps his accounts locked down tighter than Guantanamo, fortunately, his family is not as privacy savvy. I've been knee-deep in all of Isaac's family photos that span the last two decades—from college football games, family weddings, holidays, and births, to every vacation he and Brianna have taken.

I spend long moments dwelling on their last trip, snorkeling in Costa Rica for a spring break. They stayed in a tropical villa nestled in a private beach cove, and it's undoubtedly the most romantic thing I've ever seen. Never once did Dean and I take a trip like that. And the year before, they ziplined in Puerto Rico. And the year before that, it was a floating villa in Fiji. When Isaac mentioned that Brianna was accustomed to a certain lifestyle, he wasn't exaggerating. Isaac and Brianna are picture-perfect—like they've been plucked from the pages of *Travel & Leisure* magazine.

I think back on one of the last times I saw Brianna when we were young. She and her clique of mean girls brutalized me, until the accident. Then, they just ignored me—out of guilt, I assume.

The air smells like cut grass and overpriced perfume as I sit at the edge of the schoolyard, trying to disappear into the pages of my book. It's my shield, a thin barrier between me and the world, but it's not thick enough today. Laughter erupts from the cluster of picnic tables under the cypress trees, where Brianna and her clique reign, their voices sharp and carrying even over the lunchtime chatter.

I can feel Brianna's eyes on me before she even starts walking over, her heels clicking against the pavement like an ominous countdown. Her friends trail behind her, a perfectly choreographed entourage in designer clothes and sneers that cost more than my entire wardrobe. Shame burns red hot on my cheeks. Can she tell Isaac and I were intimate? Can she see that her ex-boyfriend's hands were sliding over my bare skin just a few nights ago as we cocooned ourselves under the blankets in his bed?

"There she is, the charity case herself," Brianna announces as they circle me, blocking my sunlight. Her voice is syrupy sweet, like poison wrapped in silk. "Shae, still pretending to read? We all know you're too stupid to understand that book."

I keep my eyes down, focusing on a word—any word—hoping they'll get bored and leave. But today, Brianna is on a roll, fueled by an audience that hangs on her every malicious word.

"Why are you even here, Shae? Your dad can barely pay the rent, and you think you can hang out with us? You should just disappear. Honestly, you would do everyone a favor," she spits out, her followers giggling like this is the best entertainment they've had all week. I feel the heat rising in my cheeks, my hands clenching around my book so tightly, it might tear.

"Leave me alone, Brianna," I manage to say, my voice low but firm.

Brianna steps closer, her face inches from mine, her breath smelling like mint and malice. "Or what? You'll cry? Run back to your trashy trailer park? You're so pathetic."

"Surprised you haven't run away from home yet like your mom did," another chimes in.

Her friends snicker, and someone adds, "You should just kill yourself."

The words are a punch to the gut, stealing my breath. It's one thing to endure the daily digs about my clothes, my family's lack of money, but this . . . this is something darker, more dangerous. It echoes inside me, a dark whisper that frightens me even as I push it away. Dad and his new girlfriend have decided I should start seeing a therapist to handle my anger issues, but all of my issues are born of their cruelty. I want to kill them. All of them.

Brianna's laugh cuts through the haze of my shock. "Look at her, she's about to cry. What a joke."

I stand up suddenly, my chair scraping loudly against the concrete. I need to escape, to breathe air that isn't thick with their cruelty. "I'm not a joke," I say, my voice stronger now, louder. "You think you're better than me because your parents have money? That doesn't make you better. It just makes you luckier."

For a moment, Brianna looks taken aback, her mask slipping to reveal a flicker of insecurity. But it's gone as quickly as it appeared, replaced by a cold, hard glare. "Whatever, Shae. Keep telling yourself that if it makes you feel better. Come on, let's leave the trash to rot."

They turn away, their laughter trailing behind them like the tail of a comet, bright and burning and meant to destroy anything in its path. I sit back down, my heart still pounding, my hands shaking. The words they threw at me linger in the air, ghosts that refuse to be silent. But I open my book again, forcing myself to focus on the words, on worlds where right triumphs and bullies are just villains waiting to be defeated.

Today, I didn't disappear. I didn't let them erase me. And maybe that's a small victory, a tiny act of defiance against the Briannas of the world. But it's mine, and for now, it's enough.

"Oh, Kelly . . ." I breathe into the steamy air, shaking the dark memories away. *"What would you do?"*

I swish my hand through the soapy bathwater as I conjure Kelly's kind face in my mind. "I'm sure you'd say something profoundly simple." I try to think my way around my current situation. It's difficult being Kelly and still holding Shae in my psyche. I've basically abandoned the girl I was in favor of my future, but Shae lingers like a bad boyfriend. "Shae, do you think you're trying to relive the past in the hope of changing the outcome?"

I scrunch my nose, pretending Kelly is seated across from me, a kind, expectant smile on her face.

"Well, Kelly . . ." I say aloud, attempting to play both roles in this make-believe therapy session. "I . . ." I can't find the words to answer her. "I . . . want a redo," I say into the silence. "I want to make him pay for taking everything from me." I gulp down a painful ball in my throat. "And I want him to love me like he loves her."

I splash the water over the edge of the tub as I admit that last part. I'm trying to be aware of not repeating cycles, and chasing Isaac just to steal him away from his wife sounds like a road I've traveled before. A few times. No, I'm not here to steal Isaac from anyone. I'm here to right some wrongs.

I don't know if Isaac knows how my life changed after he made his exit back then, but something in me wants him to know, wants him to feel the pain he inflicted on me firsthand.

Am I looking for revenge? Not exactly. All I want is some awareness, maybe an acknowledgment on his part that his bad decisions carved a path of destruction far beyond what he realized. And if anything, this reconnection and his life now are proof enough that he carried on thriving, while I nearly drowned in despair.

A wicked sense of resentment crawls over my skin as I stare into Isaac's captivating eyes looking back at me from his profile photo. An idea strikes me then—a way to insert myself in his life without his even realizing. It might even help me get a better handle on his therapy sessions going forward. I log out of my Facebook account and then instantly hit the "sign up for a new account" button. I type in an old email address that I never use anymore and then punch in the name of one of the football players from Santa Cruz High who would have played with Isaac.

"This is definitely *not* what Kelly would do." I smirk as I hit the "create new account" button. A minute later, I'm uploading a generic photo of the mascot from our high school for my new profile picture. I punch in "Santa Cruz High School" to the About Me section of my new profile and then spend a couple minutes sending friend requests to a few people who also graduated from Santa Cruz High around the same time Isaac and I did. And another moment after that, I'm sending a friend request to the man of the hour—Isaac Rawlins.

It doesn't take long for the notifications to start lighting up my screen. By the time my fingertips are the texture of prunes, Facebook is notifying me that Isaac and I are now friends. I have full access to his life, and he's making it so simple. If he only knew the truth— that I am not the woman he thinks I am. I'm his worst nightmare dressed as his therapist, complete with bloodred lips and acrylic nails sharp enough to maim and kill. Just like a spider spinning a silky-soft web, I'll lure Isaac in with the promise of a sparkly new toy; he won't even know he's trapped until it's too late.

I'm just scrolling through the last few years of Isaac's life in profile photos when the idea percolates to life that I should take an evening walk down the cul-de-sac tonight. With any luck, I'll be able to get a peek into their home life. Do they make dinner together? Does

Brianna curl up on the couch with Isaac when he watches football games? I'm suddenly obsessed with the notion of catching a glimpse inside their private time.

Just once. Just to see.

A stubborn memory I haven't thought of since I was a kid materializes.

The sound of clattering dishes. Loud laughter. The scrape of a chair on linoleum.

"Well, what do we have here?" Her throaty, cigarette-rough voice rings through the kitchen. The women always smell like beer and something else I can't quite place. One of my father's stained T-shirts hangs off one shoulder, and she isn't wearing anything else.

"Need a little midnight snack, sweetie?" Her smile is wide and warm. I can see she's missing a tooth. Her skin is the texture of the cracked vinyl in my father's car. "Don't you talk?"

I remain still, unwilling to give this strange woman my words.

"Woman!" my father bellows through the house. He comes around the corner a moment later, eyes landing on me. "Whaddyu doin' up? Thought I locked your door before I left earlier."

The woman's face remains unchanged, as if she didn't just witness my father confessing to child abuse and neglect. I don't mind though. The closet is my safe space now. Alone in my closet is the only place I wanna be when life is falling apart.

"Go on." Dad gestures at me to head back upstairs. I clamp down my teeth until pain radiates through my jaw. I swallow the ball of tears that tightens in my throat. Rage bubbles to life, but I tamp it down. Rage won't get me anywhere. I need to think smart. By the time I turned seven, I knew I had more kindness and logic than the man who raised me. By eight, I knew I was on my own in life, no one to depend on but myself. My father clears his throat, annoyance creeping in. "Go on, girl."

Pain twists and turns my insides. "I'm hungry!"

His eyes shoot up with surprise. He's not used to me yelling back at him, but I'm eight now. I know it's not okay that he leaves me without food all day. The teachers at school told us at the assembly last week that if anyone—including our parents—ever made us feel threatened or hurt us, we should tell a teacher or another adult we trust. But I don't trust anyone more than my dad, and anyway, does making me skip dinner because I didn't clean my room count as hurting someone? I'm not sure. But I know he can't starve me forever. Even if there isn't anything other than ramen and peanut butter and jelly sandwiches to eat, I know I'll be able to fill up my tummy at school. He can't keep us from going to school. He already tried that when he forgot to unlock the closet door one morning before he left for work. The principal called him and asked where we were. He hasn't forgotten about us since that day.

"You can wait till breakfast, girl. Go on up," Dad instructs again. My stomach growls in protest, but I do as I'm told.

Before I climb the stairs to my room, I turn to see him swat at her bare bottom under his old T-shirt. My heart feels like it just caught fire in my chest. I'd do anything for the attention he gives this strange woman who smells like cigarettes. I'd do anything for his loving gaze to land on me like that. I'd even kill for the kindness he doles out to Sophie so easily.

So why isn't my love enough?

A series of loud bangs echoes through the cottage and pulls me from my thoughts. Fear spikes in my bloodstream before I take a few deep breaths and push myself out of the tub. I wrap myself in a fuzzy white robe and then pad down the hallway to the front door. With beads of sweat and steam still covering my face, I open the door to find a young guy smiling back at me.

"Welcome to the neighborhood. I'm Taylor."

CHAPTER 10

"So, how long have you been helping the crazies?" Taylor pulls from his bottle of kombucha as we sit talking on the front porch.

"Come again?" I half laugh but also take offense.

"How long have you been a therapist?" His brown-eyed gaze sparkles, and the tone of his voice is playful. I usually make a point of not getting attached to people, but I'm surprised to find I like this one. We've been chatting on the front step of the cottage for twenty minutes, and already, I can tell that while he speaks without a filter, he also means no harm and seems to do it only to see if he can get a rise out of me. He's not my type—too young with a reckless air that's more turn-off than turn-on for me—but he's nothing if not entertaining.

"Days like this make me think I've been doing this job for too long," I finally quip.

"Rough day?"

"You could say that. I was soaking in the tub and then about to pour some wine before you landed on my doorstep." I smile.

"Well, don't let me stop you." He turns to me as if he's ready for me to reveal all my deepest secrets. *Where would I even start?* I think.

"I don't need it. I used to have a bottle-a-day habit. I'm trying to watch it now," I confess.

"I hear that." He swirls and then swigs his kombucha.

"Do you drink?" I ask politely.

"Nah. Just this stuff." He lifts the bottle. "I don't like the hang-over that comes with drinking. Nothing beats a joint on the beach to end the day though." He pulls a small joint from his top pocket. "You smoke?" I shake my head. "You mind if I do?" I shake my head again. "Good. We practically share a backyard. If you ever see me out in back, come on over."

"Wait, you don't live in this cul-de-sac?"

"Hell no. Too expensive for my blood. I rent the guesthouse on the property behind yours. It's hardly a guesthouse, more like an old shack, but the guy's got me paying twenty-five hundred a month for it. It's okay. I'm not paying for the roof anyway—I'm paying for the killer waves practically right out my door. I don't even have to put on sandals to walk to the beach. Having the Pacific Ocean in your front yard is priceless."

"So . . . you just drink kombucha and surf all day?"

"Basically." He shrugs. "I hit North Shore in Oahu every Janu-ary for the swells, but otherwise, I'm here." His smile is easy and inviting.

An errant thought runs through my mind that he's a potential witness—and therefore a potential problem. I can't risk attachments here. I narrowly escaped with my life from Pacific View Psychiatric. If I don't walk the tightrope and mind my p's and q's, I could find myself in a far worse cage than that one.

"Sounds like a pretty easy life," I comment.

"It is, but it wasn't always that way." He looks up to the blue sky. "I worked the gang unit for the San Francisco Police Department for nearly a decade before I decided law enforcement was not the life for me."

"Law enforcement?" I nearly choke. He nods. "You don't really look like a cop."

He lifts his eyebrows. "And what does a cop look like?"

I shrug, glancing down at his feet. "Not barefoot, I guess."

He wiggles his toes and then breaks into a warm grin. "Got me there. I turned in the uniform for a surfboard last summer and haven't looked back since."

I nod, taking in this revelation. Having a former cop for a neighbor isn't something I anticipated. "So you're probably a pretty observant guy . . ."

"Sure." He shrugs and finishes the kombucha.

"Any crazies in the neighborhood?" I laugh halfheartedly.

He shrugs. "We have a pretty active neighborhood watch, so things stay pretty peaceful." His smile is wide. "Guess that makes you the only crazy one." He winks, stands, and throws me a quick wave as he walks down my path. "Give a holler if you ever need me. I'm just a few steps away."

"Great," I mumble, suddenly cursing the neighborly *Wonder Years* vibe Carmel has. This would have been the perfect spot for Kelly, but for me? I couldn't be more uncomfortable knowing that *everyone* is watching.

CHAPTER 11

We're sitting in Isaac's muscle car, parked at our usual spot overlooking the city. The sun dips below the horizon, setting the sky on fire with shades of orange and pink. It should be perfect. It's the sort of moment I've come to cherish since we started dating. But Isaac's got this look on his face, the one that says he's wrestling with something big. I brace myself.

"Shae, there's something I need to talk to you about," he starts, his voice heavy. He's not looking at me; he's staring off into the distance, watching the sun disappear. A shiver courses through me as a flashback of the night Isaac took my virginity comes back to me. I relive that night in my mind often, my first taste of sweet pleasure.

I nod, keeping my face neutral. "What's up?"

He takes a deep breath. "It's Brianna," he says, and just like that, the warmth of the setting sun feels a little colder.

I feel a knot tighten in my stomach, but I manage to keep my voice steady. "What about her?"

Isaac finally turns to look at me, his eyes earnest. "She's going through a really tough time right now. Her parents are getting a divorce, and it's messy. She's kind of falling apart."

Part of me wants to say, good, but the better part of me bites my tongue. Brianna's made my life hell for as long as I can remember. It's *hard to muster up any sympathy for the girl who's taunted and bullied me, who's made me feel like I'm worth less than the dirt under her expensive shoes.*

"She's changed, Shae," Isaac continues, oblivious to the storm of emotions inside me. "She's not the same person she was at the beginning of the summer. She's . . . softer, more vulnerable."

I almost laugh. Soft? Vulnerable? This is Brianna we're talking about, right? The same Brianna who last week told me I'd be pretty too if I could afford some decent clothes?

Isaac is still talking, and I force myself to focus. "She asked me to go to a concert with her. It's this band I've told you about, the one I really like. The show's sold out. She got the tickets before . . . everything happened."

I stare at him, feeling like he's just dropped a cold stone into my stomach. "So, you're going?" I manage to ask.

He nods. "Yeah, I think I should. Just as friends. She needs someone right now, and I know her better than anyone. We've got history, Shae."

History. *The word hangs in the air between us like a fog. I think about my own history—my mom leaving, my dad's drinking, my sister always needing more than I have to give. I think about the hope that had started to build inside me these last few months with Isaac. Hope that feels like it's slipping through my fingers now.*

"It's just one night, Shae," Isaac says, as if reading my thoughts. "It doesn't change how I feel about you."

But it does, doesn't it? It changes everything. I want to scream, to tell him that he's making a mistake, that Brianna is using him. But what if I'm wrong? What if she really is going through a hard time? What if I'm just being the jealous girlfriend?

I look away from Isaac, out over the city lights that twinkle like distant stars. At least he's being honest and upfront with me, I think. It would be easier for him to just lie to me, but he's not doing that.

"I understand," I say, and I hate how weak my voice sounds. "You should be there for her. She's lucky to have you."

Isaac smiles, relief flooding his features. "Thank you, Shae. I knew you'd understand. You're amazing, you know that?"

Am I? Or am I just a pushover?

He pulls me into a hug, and I let myself lean into him, breathing in the familiar scent of his cologne. For a moment, I let myself pretend that everything is okay, that the girl he's going to see his favorite band with isn't the same one who's made it her mission to make my life miserable.

But as we pull apart and Isaac starts the car, ready to take me home, the reality settles back in. Brianna and Isaac have a past, a connection that I can't understand. Maybe they are meant for each other, two sides of the same golden coin. But all I can think is, What about us?

And maybe, just maybe, I need to start thinking about my own future, one where I don't come second to the ghost of a relationship that refuses to die.

As Isaac drives, I watch the city pass by, each streetlight a reminder that the world is moving on, with or without me. And I decide, maybe for the first time, that I need to start moving on too.

CHAPTER 12

I'm stewing. Brianna Rawlins obviously believes her own time to be more valuable than mine. If she only knew what I was up to when she's not around. I smirk. I like the feeling that I have one up on the woman who has it all. A beautiful face, a beautiful husband, a beautiful home . . . everything about her is enviable. But where she's lacking is where I excel. My clever determination has gotten me further in life than she'll ever go, and I'm about to teach her just how much that matters.

I straighten Kelly's string of pearls at my neck. The elegant Peter Pan collar that they accent lends me a polished, Stepford Wife vibe that comes surprisingly naturally to me. While life in LA with Dean was always about who you knew and where you were going for dinner, life in Carmel is slower and sweeter, and suddenly, it has me thinking about what a life with Isaac would look like here. Sun-soaked walks on the beach and lazy summer days drinking homemade lemonade in the backyard. I find myself wanting things with Isaac that I've never wanted with another man. I want to be better, be the wife he deserves. My chance was stolen from me back then, but now that opportunity is knocking again, I feel more ready than ever to take back what has always been mine.

I glance down at my—*correction*, Kelly's—Cartier watch. I was surprised to find it nestled deep in the velvet recesses of her jewelry drawer. It's not something I ever saw her wear, but then, when would she have a chance to wear it? With no one to take her out on fancy dates and no pretentious socialite friends to check out the latest hot-spot eatery, of course it would languish in a corner collecting dust. All of Kelly's life was spent languishing and collecting dust, from the looks of it. We like to believe that everyone has a more interesting life than us—that just beneath the surface, there are things we don't know, mysteries to discover. But I'm finding with Kelly, what you see is what you get—and what you get is about as boring as watching paint dry.

She only reads nonfiction books if the titles occupying her book-shelf are any indication, watches true crime docuseries on Netflix, based on her browsing history, and vacations at Clearwater Beach, Florida, every single spring without fail. Kelly's life is as cookie-cutter as it comes. She's the kind of woman I've lived my life both envying and resenting in the same breath.

I sigh, realizing Brianna is now ten minutes late for our first indi-vidual session. Would it be a red flag if I terminated our relation-ship? She has no respect for my time, and if I've learned one thing in this new gig, it's that time is money.

Frustration sizzles through my veins as I think about how easy it was to pad my bank account when I was an online influencer. A little tragedy goes a long way toward boosting the Patreon and GoFundMe bank deposits. Now, I actually have to work for the money.

Thankfully, Kelly's hourly rate is astronomical; inflation is gnarly on the California coast. I'll give Kelly that—she was determined and driven enough for two decades to charge an arm and a leg at this stage of her career, and for that, I'm grateful.

The office doorbell chimes. I straighten my spine, suck in a breath, and then move through the house quickly to open the office door. I don't bother to hide my annoyance at her tardiness.

Brianna smiles back at me with a toothy grin. I suppress a cringe when I look down to find she's holding two bowls of fresh fruit. "I'm sorry I'm late. I brought snacks!"

She sidles past, and a wave of her perfume hits me. Instantly, the thought of banning heavy perfumes in my office comes to me. I bite back the urge to say something, because she did bring snacks, after all.

"How are things going?" I say instead.

"Great." She beams back at me. I don't reply because she wouldn't be sitting in front of me if things were so great. "Well, just okay, I guess," she finally admits, plucking a slice of cantaloupe from one bowl and setting the other on the table that separates us. I settle in the chair, open my notebook, and write the current date on the top of the page.

"How are things going, really?" I say quietly.

"Isaac ignores me constantly. All he talks about is work, and he spends his free time working out or on the golf course with the boys. He doesn't even pretend to love me anymore." Her pouty lips are shaped into a perfect bow, and I wonder how much filler she's had to keep them looking freshly plumped.

"Marriages can be tricky to navigate. You've been together how long?" I pretend to scratch notes.

"Since we were fourteen. Almost twenty years," she states. I flinch at the reminder they were together the summer we were together. The timelines intertwine; I knew it then, but it still causes a sting. Was he playing both of us at the same time? It seems like that, but he was my first boyfriend—and he wasn't even that. He was the first boy I ever thought I could love, so that's something, right? Apparently, Brianna thought the same thing, because here she is, still loving him, while I'm pretending to be someone else.

"Fourteen, that's very young."

"You think you know so much at that age." Her grin is rueful.

"And the older you get, you realize you know nothing at all." I shift, allowing my eyes to scan her form as she plucks at the hem of her snow-white cardigan. She's naturally elegant. She always has been. The line of her swanlike neck, the creamy flesh that glistens with a sun-kissed California glow. Her shoulder-length honey-blonde hair is shaped into loose waves with the help of a curling wand and a lot of product. Her makeup is natural—beige-pink lips and just a swipe of blush and eyeshadow. She radiates some sort of inner glow that I've never once had and I'm sure can't be purchased in a bottle.

It makes me hate her more, the way she moves through life with such effortless beauty. It's obvious what Isaac sees in her. She has a presence that draws people in, and I am one of those people. My memories of our high school years are spotty at best, and for good reason, but what I do remember is Brianna as homecoming queen, standing next to Isaac. Brianna winning state finals in track and field. Brianna starring in the school production of *Grease*. If you didn't know Brianna back then, you weren't paying attention.

And I always pay attention.

"I love that shade of red lipstick on you. It's so striking. I could never pull that off." Brianna smiles sweetly, and my stomach churns.

"Thanks," I hum. "I picked it up at Chanel last week. I'm not sure it's for me either, but the salesclerk twisted my arm."

"It's great. It really pops on you. The most color I get is from a sunburn." Her laugh is light and airy.

"Well, thank you for saying so." I draw little pentagrams around Brianna's name as I think about what to say next. "It's good to try new things, I guess."

"Yeah," she says, eyes lingering on mine. "Are you a member of the country club? I could get you in with a guest pass—we should go for cocktails. Happy hour with a view of the ocean! But don't let the term 'happy hour' fool you. The drinks are still overpriced. Strong though." She pops a sliced strawberry into her mouth. "Are you married, Doctor?"

My eyebrows shoot up my forehead as I marvel at how brazen she is. "No. Never."

"Why?"

"*Why*, what?" I ask, put off by her nosiness.

"You just haven't found the right guy? They must be falling at your feet. Oh . . . I guess I shouldn't assume." She frowns. "You haven't found the right guy or girl?"

I smile at her insinuation that I might be gay. Does this red lipstick really make me look like a power lesbian? I don't mind if it does; putting people off is my main priority.

"I'm not really looking. Life happens when you're busy making other plans, right?"

"Right. Well, I vote we have our next session at the country club. Do you know how to golf?"

"Golf? Yeah. I love golfing." My lie is smooth.

"Great. I can introduce you to some very eligible bachelors. Maybe we'll even get lucky and catch you a husband! Or *wife* . . . if that's your thing."

"I haven't dated in a long time. I had a bad experience a few years ago that left me with a suitcase full of trauma," I offer lightly.

"Well, you know what they say—the best way to get over a man is to get under another one."

"Is that what they say?" I chuckle.

"Sounds good to me." Her eyes sparkle with mischief.

It's too bad Brianna Rawlins said *I do*, because when she did, she signed her death certificate.

CHAPTER 13

"What would Kelly do?" I hum.

Brianna has been gone for six hours, and I've spent all of them deep-diving the internet. I've found their marriage license, thanks to the Santa Cruz courthouse digitizing their records last year. A quick glance at local property assessments reveals exactly which house is theirs at the end of the cul-de-sac, and a hop over to Zillow tells me everything about their home—the layout, the updated kitchen and primary bath, right down to their most recent tax bill and the price they paid for it. There isn't much else to be found on Isaac and Brianna. They've lived a private life, I'll give them that, but that doesn't make them untraceable. No one is nowadays.

I also stumbled across a random Reddit article claiming that Shae Halston, *internet influencer and murderer*—I roll my eyes as I read—has been moved to San Luis Psychiatric in Pismo Beach. My heart butterflies wildly as I consider what this means for Kelly. For *me*. A brief internet search informs me that San Luis Psychiatric is one of the best-rated psychiatric hospitals in California. I spend the next thirty minutes looking for any confirmation that Kelly has, in fact, been moved, but I find nothing.

I think back on one of my first sessions with Kelly after I created the Mia Starr brand.

The office smells faintly of lavender and lemon, an attempt at calm, I suppose, but it does nothing to soothe the storm inside me. Kelly sits across from me, her posture relaxed yet attentive, a soft smile on her lips that doesn't quite reach her eyes. I know she sees through people, through their facades, but not mine. Not today.

I start with the basics, my voice steady, confident. "Things have been really amazing lately. My online following has exploded. I'm practically a celebrity now." I flick my hair back, a practiced gesture of nonchalance.

Kelly nods, scribbling something in her notepad. "That sounds exciting, Shae. Tell me more about that. What's it been like managing your growing fame?"

It's my cue to embellish, to paint my life in the vibrant hues of success. "Oh, it's been fantastic. The fans, the virtual events, the sponsorships! It's like a whirlwind of excitement. Just last week, I was invited to an exclusive launch party. Everyone wanted to be seen with me." The words taste bitter in my mouth, the lie thick on my tongue.

Kelly's eyes are thoughtful, probing even. "That sounds quite fulfilling. How does all of this affect your personal life? Last time we talked about some challenges there."

Personal life. The term feels foreign, a land I've long since left. "Well, you know, my husband has been so supportive. He really is my rock." I laugh, a hollow sound that echoes around the room. In truth, he checked out on us months ago, couldn't stand the shadow of fame—or so I tell myself.

Kelly leans forward slightly, her expression unchanged. "It's wonderful to have such support. How often does he join you for these events?"

The question catches me off guard. "Oh, you know, he's a busy man. Works a lot. But he's always there when it matters." Another lie. He's never there because there are no events. And even if there were, I'd have to decline them because I never show my face on my social media pages.

"And how do you balance your time between this rapid professional growth and your relationship?" Kelly asks, her tone gentle, almost coaxing.

I shift in my seat, uneasy. "Balance is key, of course. We make sure to have quality time. Dinners, vacations . . ." I trail off, thinking of the silent apartment, the dinners eaten alone while he works late. Sometimes we attend his work events together, but mostly, it's just me, spending my days alone.

Kelly's silence is heavy, filled with unspoken questions. "Shae, last session, you mentioned some difficulties in your marriage. Has there been a change since then?"

I stiffen, my facade cracking. "Changes? Well, yes, improvements mostly. We're better than ever." My voice is too bright, too forced. I'm a master of my own reality, aren't I?

Kelly doesn't look convinced, but she doesn't push. Instead, she shifts the topic subtly. "It's important to have a support system, especially with such a demanding career. Besides your husband, who else do you confide in?"

My mind races. Confide? The very word feels alien. "I have loads of friends—countless, really. Everyone loves being around me." I think of the friends who have drifted away over the years.

"That's good to hear," Kelly says, though her eyes are sad. "It's essential to keep those connections alive and genuine."

Genuine. The word stings, a sharp rebuke dressed in a velvet glove. I nod, though my heart pounds with the fear of being discovered, of being seen as less than what I project.

"We're almost out of time today," Kelly remarks, closing her notepad. "But I'd like you to think about something for our next session. Consider what 'genuine' means to you, in your relationships and your career."

I nod again, a mechanical puppet on strings of falsehoods. As I stand to leave, the room feels smaller, or maybe I do. The door closes behind me, and I step back into the world, one where I am famous and fabulous, ignoring the echo of emptiness that follows me out.

I tear myself from the memory, close my laptop, and set it aside. Ants crawl through my veins as the urge to do *something* overtakes me. I finish the last of my red wine and then curl a soft, creamy knit blanket around my shoulders and walk out to the front porch. Darkness has already descended, and the small bungalows cast long shadows around the neighborhood. I tuck the blanket tighter around my shoulders to fend off the ocean breeze. I've seen Isaac walk his dog in this direction a dozen times, but I've never let my eyes linger long enough to determine which house he lives in. But thanks to local property records, now I know.

The street winds gently around a small grouping of orange trees. My eyes travel to the end of the cul-de-sac in search of Isaac's house. Carmel is unique in that it doesn't have traditional addresses or mailboxes. In an effort to keep the town quaint, residents have voted to forgo house numbers. Quaint or not, it makes it much more difficult to navigate, especially when I'm in search of one very specific house. Lush landscaping, neatly trimmed lawns lined with creeping ivy, and citrus trees provide a layer of privacy between the idyllic gingerbread-style bungalows. Is this what my life would have been if Isaac and I had never broken up all those years ago? I haven't thought about all the what-ifs in so long—mostly because I've been too busy dealing with Mia Starr and Dean and all the baggage that comes with that life. But now, I can feel seeds of envy embedding themselves in my heart.

I blink away a painful memory of that summer, the summer I turned sixteen. The last time I ever laid eyes on the sharply drawn angles of Isaac's face feels like so long ago. It's strange when the life you never had flashes before your eyes. With him, anything felt possible. The last time we were together, I hung on his every word. I still am, ironically. Only now, I get paid for it. What would he do if he knew exactly who he was revealing his darkest thoughts to? I remember the last night we were together back then, his hands under my sweater as we kissed on the pier at midnight. Little did I know that by dawn two days later, my life would be turned upside down—my sister, gone. My good half, stolen. My heart, hardened.

A dog barking yanks me from my memories. I glance up, finding I've stopped right at Isaac and Brianna's house.

A shiny black Toyota pickup is parked in the driveway, and his dog is staring at me through the front windows of the cottage. It's Isaac's dog. I'm sure of it. My gaze crawls around the yard, and a garden statue in the shape of a seagull in flight catches my eye only because it's so kitsch. Flowering vines of purple ivy cling to the doorways and windows. The pitched roof is enchanting. This cottage has way more charm than Kelly's boring white bungalow with sunshine-yellow shutters. Based on the sale history, I know that Isaac and Brianna bought it ten years ago for a pretty penny—and the real estate market in this area has only ballooned since then. I haven't had a chance to look up the sale price of Kelly's cottage, mostly because she's only renting it, so it doesn't really matter. But if I had to guess, I'd bet Kelly's house is half the price of Isaac's. Where his house is on the larger side for the cottages in this neighborhood, Kelly's is by far the smallest.

I don't know much about Isaac's business, but from the outside, it looks like they're doing well. As I recall from the layout on Zillow, a formal sitting area is located in the front of the house—where Isaac's dog is looking at me from right now. A dining room and kitchen follow, and across the hall is the large informal living room and two guest bedrooms. Upstairs, a spacious, open primary bedroom and bath, featuring floor-to-ceiling windows that boast a view of the ocean, encompass the entire top floor, and a full unfinished basement sits below the main floor. The lot is nearly an acre of mature fruit trees and formal hedges that wind along stone pathways, and there's a koi pond. Isaac and Brianna's home looks like it fell out of a fairy tale, so what happened to their happily-ever-after?

It occurs to me that I can't just linger around Isaac's house. A neighbor will call and report a strange peeping tom wrapped in an old woman's blanket. An idea comes to me then, and I shove a hand in the pocket of my pants and locate my receipt from the wine bar I stopped at for lunch today. I move casually to the driver's side of Isaac's truck, open the door, and then shove the little receipt in the cupholder. I close the door and am moving away as quickly as I arrived, walking with slow steps as the cul-de-sac winds in a little circle and sets me back in the direction of Kelly's cottage again.

I walk slowly by Kelly's cottage, lost in my own thoughts as I make my way to the stone path that leads down the small cliff to the beach lined with cypress trees. Only people who live in this community are supposed to have access to this beach path, but I've been here just a few weeks and have already seen high schoolers sneaking up and down the trail in the evenings, the smell of weed in the air. Or maybe it was just Taylor and his friends.

I reach the bend in the path that curves through boulders and loose stone down to the beach before I stop and take in the moonlight sparkling like crystals on the waves. The warm breeze is heavy with the scent of bougainvillea and something else. A woman's perfume. My spine straightens as it occurs to me that I'm not alone.

"Isaac . . ." Brianna's giggle carries on the wind right to my ears.

A shiver courses through me as I hear the deep baritone of his voice right down to the tips of my toes. I push aside long-forgotten memories triggered by this man as the sounds of sex fill the air. My mouth drops open as I back away a few steps and tuck myself behind the trunk of a giant cypress, shocked that I've just stumbled into an intimate moment between them. Soft grunts and willowy sighs fill the air as the uncomfortable feeling of voyeurism overcomes me. I blink away the memory of Dean and Jesika in this same situation—me watching calmly as they fucked. Some perverse part of me enjoys the control I have over them in this moment, so vulnerable and unaware that I'm lurking right here, a spider weaving its web in wait.

And then a darker thought occurs to me. I can use this moment to my advantage. Now that I know that they have this sort of relationship—one based on sexual needs above emotional ones—I can suggest something wild. Maybe an open arrangement to explore their fantasies outside of their romantic relationship. The Isaac I knew was a hunter on and off the field, a football all-star and all-American boy with an inflated ego and the insatiable desire to conquer.

Wanting Isaac in high school wasn't so much because we were the perfect fit—if I'm honest, I didn't even know him that well. I realize now that's because he didn't *want* me to. Isaac's mystique relies on smoke and mirrors.

Women are often warned about men who lie. But what about the ones who say little and let their actions speak louder? Some men don't need to lie to women. If they charm them enough, women will lie to themselves and fill in the gaps with the characteristics of their ideal lover. That's what Isaac did to me, charmed me with his intensely green gaze and a roguish, crooked grin. He didn't have to say much, just a few well-placed words and a touch here and there, and I was smitten.

My first love. Also, my last.

The truth remains that Isaac and Brianna ruined me, and they don't even know the half of it. But they will; I'll make sure of that.

I continue to move away from the beach path, walking slowly as I make my way back to my cottage. When I get there, I tuck the blanket a little tighter around my shoulders and sit down on the porch steps, unwilling to leave the glow of the soft moonlight just yet.

I wish I could bring Mia Starr back. Isaac would be a gorgeous addition to my brand. He fits the mold way more than Dean ever did. That's why I never shared Dean on my social media accounts. He definitely did *not* fit the Mia Starr lifestyle, but Isaac . . . Isaac is beautiful in a heart-stopping way that inspires envy in men and women.

I imagine the string of true-love posts: walking hand in hand on the beach, sunset selfies, romantic weekends away. We would be perfect together. I just need to get Isaac to see it too. He's already looking for an out from his marriage. I can see it in the way his eyes travel over my body while I sit across from him during our sessions.

Isaac is bored with his life, and I am more than happy to be his distraction. I plan on unraveling his perfect life one thin thread at a time. It's less than five minutes later that I see Isaac and Brianna cresting the top of the beach path and walking down our quiet street. I shrink into the shadows in the hope that I'll remain unseen.

No such luck, because as soon as they reach my house, Brianna waves and smiles at me. I wave back, eyes locked on the angles of Isaac's profile the entire time.

Little do they know I've just executed step one of my plan.

CHAPTER 14

The chill from the ocean breeze is nothing compared to the icy distance growing between Isaac and me as we walk along the pier. The boards creak under our feet, a constant reminder of the fragile state of things. Isaac's been off lately—distant since he and Brianna went to the concert together last week, almost like he's somewhere else entirely. It's like I'm walking beside a ghost of the boy who used to make my heart race.

He's been quiet all afternoon, but when he spots Brianna laughing with her new boyfriend walking hand in hand on the pier—a guy from his football team—his entire demeanor shifts. There's a hardness in his eyes, a clenched jaw. Jealousy isn't a good look on him, and it stirs a fire in me.

"Isaac, hey," I start, trying to draw his gaze back to me. "You wanna grab some ice cream? There's that new place that opened up at the wharf." I paint a bright smile on my face, hoping to cut through whatever fog he's walking through.

He barely glances at me, his eyes still locked on the scene behind us. "Nah, I'm not really in the mood."

His words sting, more than they should. The rejection feels personal, like a dismissal of more than just ice cream.

"Maybe we could see a movie this weekend?" I persist, my voice a little too chipper, a little too desperate.

"I'm busy this weekend," he murmurs, still not meeting my eyes. He's brushing me off, and it's starting to hurt.

"Busy," I repeat, nodding slowly. I can't stop the bitterness from seeping into my voice. *"Right."*

We continue walking, the silence between us growing heavier with each step. I try to think of something, anything, that might light up his face the way it used to. But as we pass by the rows of colorful arcade games, all flashing lights and cheerful music, it feels like they're mocking my failed attempts.

"Isaac, is something wrong? Are you mad at me?" I finally ask, stopping to face him. I need to know where I stand, even if it's going to hurt.

He sighs, running a hand through his hair. *"No, Shae, I'm not mad at you,"* he says, and the gentleness in his voice somehow makes it worse.

Then he pauses, looks out over the railing at the darkening waves. *"I just think . . . maybe this isn't working out."*

The words hit me like a physical blow. *"Not working out?"* I echo, my mind reeling.

"Yeah, I think I just need to be alone for a while. Find myself, you know?" He finally looks at me, his eyes full of something like regret—or is it relief?

I stand there, numb, the sounds of the pier fading into a dull roar in my ears. All the times I'd defended him to my friends, all the moments I'd thought we had something special, they flash through my mind in a painful montage.

"I see," I manage to say, even as something inside me threatens to shatter. I want to scream, to throw something, to make him feel just a fraction of the pain slicing through me. But I don't. Instead, I take a deep, shuddering breath.

"Okay, Isaac. If that's what you need." My voice is calm, even if every fiber of my being is shaking with hurt and rage.

He nods, awkwardly shuffling his feet. "I'm sorry, Shae."

"Me too," I whisper, not really sure what I'm apologizing for. Maybe for believing in this, in us. Maybe for not seeing the signs earlier.

As I walk away, the last rays of sunlight dip below the horizon, leaving the sky a bruised purple. I feel the tears threatening to spill over, but I force them back. I have to believe that karma will handle this, that what goes around comes around. It's the only thought that keeps the bitterness at bay.

I don't look back. I can't. Instead, I focus on the sound of the waves crashing against the pier, a chaotic yet soothing reminder that life goes on. And I will too, eventually.

Right now though, as I walk alone back to my car, the neon lights of the arcade flickering in the periphery, I let myself feel it all—the loss, the anger, the heartbreak. Tomorrow, I might believe in karma a little more. But tonight, it's just me and the cold, vast ocean, both of us churning with turmoil.

CHAPTER 15

My ex is living in Sacramento.

I close my email. Dean doesn't realize we still have a single shared email account that he forgot about. I've been logging in every month or so just to keep an eye on things—nothing much of value comes to this account, but some of our subscription notifications are still connected to this email address. Normally, that's no big deal. Until this morning, when I found a notification from Zillow with suggestions for rentals in Sacramento, based on my most recent searches. I certainly wasn't the one scoping out the Sacramento real estate market. The only other person it could be is Dean.

I grind my teeth as I consider what this means. Dean is moving on. While I am here, hustling for every dime. And who the hell does he know in Sacramento? Maybe a job opportunity. But then, why would he try to nail me for emotional distress in court, citing physical limitations and an inability to work after the accident in his garage in Chicago? His entire defense was bullshit—I recall good ol' Dean crushing pills on the console in his Audi when I found him that night. I do a quick search on the internet, looking for anything I can find about Dean in Sacramento, but come up empty. I make a mental note to keep an eye on this situation. Maybe even a trip to Sacramento is in order.

A vision of Isaac's crooked half grin appears in my mind's eye, and an involuntary smile turns my lips. Isaac is far more than a consolation prize. He makes Dean look like a sack of potatoes in comparison. I sigh, tipping the last of my coffee to my lips and letting the warmth swirl through my system, loosening my muscles and my tightly wound thoughts. Brianna is due for a session in ten minutes. I adjust one of Kelly's tennis bracelets at my wrist, apply a swipe of red lipstick, and shoot my reflection a classic smile. The white turtleneck that hugs my throat is demure, and paired with sleek navy slacks, I'm the picture-perfect professional woman. I need Brianna to trust me. I can't afford to trigger any of her insecurities and jealousies when it comes to my private sessions with her husband. I need to sink my hooks a little deeper into their life before she suspects me of anything.

Just as I walk out of the bathroom, the office doorbell rings through the house. A moment later, I'm swinging the door open and greeting Brianna.

"I think Isaac is cheating on me," she announces.

I have to swallow down the hot lump of coal that's lodged in my throat. Brianna shoves by me and walks to the sofa, flopping down on it unceremoniously before crossing her legs. She's dressed in a casual summer dress and a pair of white Nikes. She's the quintessential California beach girl. She looks like she's spent every day of her life in paradise. I have to control the snide remarks that swirl in my mind, but instead settle on, "What makes you think that?"

"He's acting weird," she confesses.

"Oh?" I situate myself across from her, notebook in my lap.

"He's just . . . not as loving as he usually is. Less attentive, more . . . something. I just can't put my finger on it. It's a feeling, ya know?"

I nod, scratching the words *paranoid about infidelity* in my notebook.

"At first, I thought I was just being insecure—looking for signs that aren't there." I nod, doodling in the margins as she speaks. "And then I found one."

"One what?" I nearly choke out the words.

"A receipt in his truck."

"A receipt?"

She nods. "From the new wine bar downtown."

"Okay . . ." Tingles erupt beneath my skin as I realize phase one of this plan is unfolding a little quicker than I expected. But I'm flexible; I can work with that. My talents are best honed under pressure.

"You don't believe me, do you?" She pouts, and I can see now how she uses her emotions to get what she wants out of Isaac. She's calculating. I can feel it. But where she's playing checkers, I'm three steps ahead playing chess.

"I'm just hesitant to make assumptions based on—"

"He would never go to that wine bar without me. We've been talking about going since it opened last month. He would have mentioned that he stopped there, at least." She sniffs and snags a tissue. "Plus, we're not having sex as much as we used to. We've had sex at least twice a day for years—*every single day*. But lately, it's been just once and sometimes not at all. Isaac has a high sex drive. If he's not getting it from me, he's definitely getting it from someone else."

I sit in stunned silence at what she's just revealed. I don't claim to be a rocket scientist, but I have been working as a therapist these last few months, so my understanding of human nature is pretty extensive. Plus, my nearly twenty years of therapy with Kelly before that have given me a far deeper understanding of the darkness of the psyche than I ever cared to know. Right now, Brianna needs validation and to trust her instincts. She's vulnerable to suggestion; that much is clear. A single receipt has her sobbing on my sofa.

I spend the next forty minutes listening with all the patience I can muster about every insecurity that Brianna has ever had. She's spoiled and unbearable, and I don't know how Isaac has made it this far with this woman.

"Hey—" I finally interrupt out of desperation. "I have an idea. Maybe we need a change of environment."

Her eyes shoot up with surprise.

I stumble forward, explaining, "I just find the office can be such an oppressive environment, psychologically speaking. Many of my clients have done better if we can decompress the experience. Really allow your thoughts the freedom to"—I struggle to find more psychobabble—"breathe."

"Oh," she chirps. "Okay."

I smile. "How about we have our next session at the country club—a nice view and maybe a cocktail to unwind. That sounds nice, right?"

"Yeah, it does." Her smile lifts for the first time since she walked into my office.

"So . . . meet you at the club next Tuesday at eleven?"

"It's a date."

I smile warmly as the vapid woman pushes herself from my couch, straightens the halter top of her dress, and then waves once before vacating my office.

And not a moment too soon.

CHAPTER 16

The hallways of Santa Cruz High always seem to narrow when Brianna and her posse glide through, laughter and sharp glances cutting the air. Today is no different. I shrink against my locker, hoping to disappear into its cold, metal door. My eyes focus on a smudge on its surface, but I can still feel her coming.

"There she is, the charity case herself," Brianna announces, her voice sugary poison. Her entourage echoes with giggles, the sound twisting inside me like a knife. I don't look up. I don't need to. Her perfume floods the space around me, a cloud of expensive citrus that makes my stomach turn.

"Hey, Shae, how's life in the gutter?" she sneers, stopping right in front of me. The hallway falls silent, spectators to the spectacle.

I force my eyes up, meeting her icy blue stare. "Just fine, Brianna. Thanks for asking."

Her laugh cuts through me, sharp and mocking. "Oh, look, she thinks she's witty. Remember when you thought Isaac actually liked you? What a joke."

The memory hits like a slap. Isaac, with his warm smiles and promises, telling me he cared—telling me things could be different. But it was all a game, a way to get back at Brianna after one of their countless

breakups. I was just a pawn, something he thought would make Bri-
anna mad. And it did, but not in the way he hoped. Not in a way that
changed anything for me.

"He was just using you to piss me off," Brianna continues, her voice
dripping with fake sympathy. "Because, let's face it, who could actually
fall for someone like you? All I had to do was spread some rumors around
school that you'd slept with half the guys on the football team—no one
wants to date a slut." She chuckles.

I clench my fists, my nails digging into my palms. I think of Kelly,
my new therapist, who told me to count to ten, to breathe deeply, to not
let my anger control me. But what does she know? She doesn't know
what it's like to lose a sister, be locked in a closet by a drunk father, or be
bullied by mean girls every day of high school.

"Must be hard, living your pathetic life," Brianna says, snapping
me back to the harsh light of the hallway. "No mom, a dad who doesn't
want you. Oh, but I forgot, you have a therapist now, right? The thera-
pist for lost causes."

Her words enrage me, boiling my blood with the injustice of it all.
Brianna doesn't know pain. She doesn't know what it's like to lie awake
at night, listening to the sound of your dad stumbling through the door,
drunk and angry.

"Brianna, just stop," I manage to choke out, my voice steady despite
the chaos inside me.

"Or what?" she taunts, stepping closer. "You'll cry? Go run to your
therapist?"

I want to scream, to let out all the pain and anger in one earth-shattering
moment. But I don't. Instead, I look at her, really look at her, and see
nothing but a sad, petty girl who uses cruelty to mask her own insecurities.

"You're right, Brianna," I say quietly. "I did see my therapist today.
And she told me something interesting. She said people who hurt others

are just trying to hide their own pain. So, tell me, Brianna, what are you so afraid of?"

For a moment, there's a flicker of something in her eyes—fear, maybe, or surprise. Then it's gone, and her mask is back in place.

"Whatever, Shae," she snaps, turning to leave. "Keep playing the victim. It's all you're good for."

As she walks away, the hallway starts to buzz again, life moving on as if nothing happened. But something did happen. Today, I didn't let her win. Today, I fought back in my own way.

And as I head to my next class, I think about Kelly's advice—about finding strength in the struggle, about turning pain into power. Maybe I'm not broken beyond repair. Maybe I just need to find a way to use the pieces to build something new.

I know I'm not there yet. I know the road ahead is long and fraught with more challenges than I can imagine. But for the first time in a long time, I feel a spark of hope flickering within me, stubborn and defiant.

Maybe, just maybe, I'm not a lost cause after all.

CHAPTER 17

"I think your wife is experiencing a mental break," I say as soon as Isaac sits down.

"Really?" His green eyes hold mine, warm and trusting. I have him. I can tell. A woman just knows these things.

"I can't be sure, but some of our sessions have been . . . interesting, to say the least." I choose my language carefully, allowing him to fill in the gaps with his own assumptions.

"I found her on the phone in the backyard the other day—she was having a whispered conversation and as soon as I walked over, she jumped and hung up—like I'd just caught her in the middle of something. And she's been hanging out with some new friends, people I don't know. She's out till late and sometimes she comes home all drunk and stumbly—it's not like her. She's always been open with me about her friends, but lately it seems like she's been keeping secrets from me . . . . And I guess I have noticed that she's been more defensive lately. Maybe even a little jealous in a way she never was before. I mean, what's to be jealous of? She's gorgeous. One of the things that drew me to her initially was how confident she always was." His eyes drop to his sneakers before he utters, "This jealousy thing is becoming a major turnoff. And the more I think about it, maybe she's the one who's cheating on me."

I don't say anything, letting his words hang between us.

"She acts like I'm fucking cheating on her. I'm not that guy. I wouldn't cheat, but the more she low-key accuses me of it, the more I just want to say fuck it and do it." His usual lighthearted smile is absent, replaced by a deep frown. "I mean, I might as well have some fun if I'm gonna get in trouble for it, right?"

I nod. Scratch on my notepad. Say nothing.

"She found some stupid receipt in my truck, and suddenly she thinks it's something. I don't even know how it got in there. I've never been to the place, but still, it doesn't matter what I say. She's convinced I did something, I guess."

I struggle to contain the grin that threatens to expose me. In a measured tone, I reply, "I didn't want to say this too soon, but after only a few solo sessions with Brianna, I have suspicions that maybe she is borderline."

"What does that mean?" he asks.

"Oh, well . . . at the core, it means she struggles to regulate her emotions. Bipolar is a term that's thrown around a lot, and left untreated, it could even devolve into paranoid schizophrenia. I wouldn't be too alarmed though. Do you think your wife would be open to medication to help control her paranoia about this?"

"You think she needs medication?" he asks, dumbstruck.

"Maybe. It couldn't hurt," I say simply. "Can I ask—are you committed to this marriage? In sickness and in health and so on?"

Isaac's eyes widen. "Damn, I . . . I don't know. I mean, that's what the vows said, right?"

I nod, recognizing a crack in his armor. Isaac isn't any more committed to Brianna than he was in high school, despite the fact that there's now a piece of paper connecting them for life. "Is that the kind of marriage you have?"

"I . . . uh . . . versus what?" His eyes are warm and pleading with me. To understand, to explain, to deliver him from the stress of his marriage.

"Well . . ." I think back to the fat manila file that contains twenty years of my mental health records in search of a word or phrase I can use to better explain this to him. "At the end of the day, I'm just not sure she's capable of the kind of relationship you want."

Isaac's silence speaks volumes. My words have hit their target. I'm getting under his skin one session at a time. Isaac and Brianna trust me, and there's grave danger in that misplaced trust. One day, with a little hindsight, they'll understand. But until then, I'll have them eating out of the palm of my hand.

I consider whether I should say these next words, finally deciding to throw caution to the wind and go for the money shot.

"Have you considered a trial separation? I don't usually advise that, but in some cases, it can really be a healthy option to allow both individuals to heal."

Isaac pushes a hand through his hair. The bright green of his eyes flickers a shade darker. I find him intoxicating, and the energy that radiates off him at all times is powerful. His virile, masculine presence steals all the air from the room, as if his very aura is too big to be contained in this tiny space.

"I . . . just . . . can't even process this right now." He shoves his hand through his hair again. It's a nervous gesture, I realize now, but a very sexy one. If this is Isaac stressed, I would gladly do whatever it takes to keep him in this seductive state every day.

"I'm sorry. I should have warned you before just spouting something like that."

"It's okay." His eyes search the space until they land on the clock that hangs on the wall above the door. He's looking for an out. I can see it in his eyes.

"Would you like a drink? I just opened a pinot. I won't be able to finish it before it goes bad."

"Sure." The tone of his voice is dejected. I hate that it's my fault, but the fact remains that he needs to hear it.

I set my notebook in my chair and leave, making quick work of pouring two glasses of the red wine before glancing in the mirror to make sure I look the part. My hair cascades in soft waves down over my shoulder. The spaghetti strap of my lace-trimmed camisole tends to fall down one shoulder, but I think that's a good thing. I want Isaac to notice that I'm a little undone. The dark skirt that clings to my hips is a little short on me, and when I cross my legs, the hem rides up to a very unprofessional height on my bare thigh. While I'm with Brianna, my goal is to dress every part the professional working woman, but when Isaac is here, I want to be as suggestive as possible but in a young, nearly innocent sort of way. Men like Isaac are easy to manipulate. They're all visual, and with a little ego-stroking and a few well-placed gestures, they can be controlled effortlessly. "I bet you're the only house on the block that doesn't have an ocean view," Isaac comments once I've returned.

"Oh, I do." I pass him his glass. "Only from the balcony upstairs. Wanna see?"

He doesn't say anything but follows me out of the office, down the hall, and then up the stairs to my bedroom. A strange shiver courses through me just having him here. This feels intimate, maybe like we're even crossing some sort of line. But then, that's the point— to get him thinking about the two of us here, together. Naked.

"There's that million-dollar view," he mumbles. Sips. Swirls the wine in the glass. Sips again.

"I'm a lucky lady." My gaze crawls over his broad, muscled shoulders. I wonder if he remembers Shae at all. We're different people now, without a doubt, but is there even a drop of similarity that might trigger some lost memory for him? Does he remember that night like I do? Or is his perception of the events different from mine? A part of me wants to believe he remembers. How could he forget when I never did? But I know that, most likely, he's long forgotten that night. I know I would have if I could have.

"So how are you liking Carmel?" He turns, sits in one of the lounge chairs, and then looks up at me.

Holding his gaze for even a moment feels like touching fire. My brain fails to function as something sparks to life between us.

"I love it," I say, because I can't say anything else.

"Where did you say you moved from?" His eyes follow mine as I lower myself into the chair beside him. I cross my legs and see his gaze flicker down to my creamy, exposed thigh. The golden flecks of his green eyes are bright and mischievous again. They crawl over my body as if he's gazing upon a fine work of art, appreciating the dips and curves like an artist.

"I've lived a little of everywhere. Chicago, Tahoe, LA," I answer.

"Interesting," he says, but the way he's looking at me makes me think he doesn't have my past on his mind at all.

"Do you really think a separation is the best way forward for us?" he hums. Finishes his wine. Sets the glass on the table. Shifts toward me.

"It's something to consider. Sometimes, the only relationship we should be in is the one we have with ourselves." I repeat something Kelly used to say.

"Mm-hmm." A low grunt escapes him and sends another wave of awareness through me. This man knows the effect he has on women; I have no doubt about that. "I'd be lying if I said I didn't think about it once in a while."

"I think most married couples do. It's normal."

"Mm-hmm," is his only reply.

My stomach drops when he shifts even closer to me, one fingertip grazing my bare knee. The way he uses so few words but communicates with his eyes is different from any man I've known before. It gives me the feeling of being watched. Of being hunted. Of being caught in the cage of his gaze. I am trapped, flailing to remain in control in the presence of a man who is the boss in all things he does. I've never given up control to anyone, but with him . . . I'm tempted.

"I saw you the other night." His voice is heavy, thick with innuendo.

"W-when?" I ask, barely above a whisper.

"At the cliff. When Brianna and I were fucking."

My heart clambers to a halt. "On my porch?"

"No, on the cliff path. You were watching."

"N-no, I wasn't—"

"It's okay. I don't care. That's the risk of public sex, right? Getting caught makes it hotter. I'm just glad it was you and not Gerry—that man will call the police over a shadow." Isaac rolls his eyes. "I didn't tell Brianna, if you were wondering."

I swallow, embarrassment warming my cheeks.

"Have you ever had sex on the beach?" His sideways grin deepens.

"Uh . . . no, I guess not," I say.

He moves closer. Plants both palms on my knees. He runs his thumbs in circles around the tender spot, causing a wave of ticklish sensation to hum to life. "We should change that."

"We should?" I can barely get out the words.

He only nods. The crooked grin deepens. I am caught.

The afternoon sun casts soft patterns across Isaac's chiseled features. His sessions with me are supposed to be a place of healing, of understanding, but today, it's just a backdrop for the palpable tension between Isaac and me. The air is thick with something forbidden, something reckless.

Isaac's eyes cling to mine. I watch him, feeling a mix of anticipation and a darker, deeper thrill. It's not just about attraction; it's about settling old scores. Brianna made my high school years a living hell. Now, here in my sanctuary, I'm inches away from the sweetest revenge. I lean forward slightly, letting my shirt dip just enough to catch his eye.

Isaac swallows, his gaze flickering to mine, then away. "You're very . . . distracting," he admits, his voice husky. He's beautiful when he's vulnerable, and I can't help but enjoy the power I hold over him.

"I think it's important to explore those distractions," I murmur, placing a hand on his arm. The electricity between us is instant, undeniable.

His eyes turn a shade darker with need. "Kelly, I—"

I cut him off with a kiss. It's gentle at first, a question asked with lips and breath. But then it deepens, grows more urgent, as if we're trying to consume each other's doubts and fears. His hand finds my waist, pulling me closer, and I respond by threading my fingers through his hair, anchoring him to this moment, to me.

We break apart, breathless. "We shouldn't be here where anyone could see us," he whispers, a protest drowned out by his ragged breathing.

"But it's more fun this way," I whisper back, my voice laced with everything unspoken, everything we're risking. But I don't move away. Instead, I kiss him again, harder this time, more insistent.

He roams his hands over my back, pulling me even closer, and I can feel the heat of his skin through his shirt. My heart races, not just with desire but with the knowledge of who he is, who he belongs to. *Brianna.* It makes every touch, every kiss, sweeter, tainted with the taste of revenge.

But then, Isaac freezes, his hands stopping their exploration. He pulls back slightly, his forehead pressed against mine.

"You've got me playing with fire here," he breathes, the reality of our actions crashing down like a cold wave.

I pause, my mind racing. This is the moment of truth. I can push him away, end this now, or I can pull him back into the depths with me.

"Like a moth to a flame." My voice is soft but laced with determination. "We're careful, aren't we?"

Isaac nods, but his eyes are full of conflict. "I can't lose her . . ."

The words sting, a sharp reminder of the lines we're crossing, of the roles we're betraying. For a split second, I see the gravity of what I'm doing—playing a dangerous game with people's lives, just like mine was played with. But then the memory of Brianna, laughing as she tossed cruel words like daggers, hardens my resolve.

"I guess we should end our session for today," I say finally, pulling back to look at him. My voice is steady, my decision made—not out of care for him, but as a strategic retreat.

Isaac looks relieved and guilty all at once. He nods, standing up quickly, as if escaping the physical proximity might absolve him of his lapse. "You're right. I should go."

I watch him leave, my heart a tumult of emotions. Triumph, because I've marked the first crack in their perfect facade. Fear, because of the darkness I'm nurturing inside me. And a twisted satisfaction, knowing I'm not done yet. Not until Brianna feels just a fraction of the pain she once inflicted on me.

This man has infected me like a virus I never want the cure for.

CHAPTER 18

"Saw you last night," is the first thing Taylor says when I walk in.

"You work here?" I chuckle as Taylor stands behind the bar at Casa Vinos, a bottle of wine in each hand.

"My brother owns the place. I'm helping him out temporarily." Taylor sets the bottles on a shelf behind the bar. "He just opened a month ago, and already he's doing more business than he expected. Hard to find a good bartender in this town, so here I am, saving the day."

"Saving the day, my ass! You've just been sitting here all day, getting in my way. If I have to look at your ugly mug all day, I might as well get some work out of you."

"Meet my brother, Greg." Taylor gestures to him. "This is my neighbor Kelly."

When he says the name, I nearly stumble. I'm still not used to being a Kelly. I don't think I'll ever get used to it.

"Congratulations on the wine bar," I say to his brother.

"Why, thanks." He smiles warmly at me before disappearing into the back again.

"So where did you see me?" I sit on a barstool. The place is empty, but then, they did just open for the afternoon.

"I went surfing last night. On the walk home, I saw you with a gentleman suitor." His eyes sparkle with mischief as he enunciates the last word.

"Oh really?" A momentary sense of shock shakes me.

"Saw you on the front porch. Y'all looked pretty intense. Isn't that the guy who's going to couples therapy with his wife?"

Shit. I am caught. It was easy to get lost in the crowds of Chicago, but here, everyone knows one another. I underestimated how small small-town living could be. I assumed that the constant wave of tourists in the area would make for a solid sense of anonymity, but I was wrong. The locals are always paying attention.

"Um . . ." I press my lips together, picking up the wine menu in an effort to distract myself.

"Never mind. Don't answer that. It's not my business how you live your life. I just hope the state of California doesn't catch wind of it. Fucking the patients can't be ethical, right?" He laughs as he pours me a small glass of red wine from a carafe. "It's the house blend. Give it a try. It's good."

I nod, thankful he's not letting me hang onto his last statement about fucking the patients. I guess I didn't really consider how ethical it is. The truth is, I don't even know the rules and regulations to be licensed in California. I just waltzed right into Kelly Fraser, PhD's life and picked up where she left off. Will I need to renew my license to practice every year? Do they do an office tour? And who is *they* exactly? I haven't come across any paperwork that indicates what I'm supposed to do to keep up with Kelly's practice, and for the first time, I think I might be in over my head on this one. "This is good," I say after I sip the red.

"It's a local blend. The grapes are grown just south of here."

"I'll take a full glass of it." I smile, sliding my empty glass his way. He pours more, then sets the carafe next to us and leans in.

The golden hues of sunset cast a soft glow over the wine bar, bathing the place in a picturesque light that could be straight out of a travel magazine. I sip my wine, savoring the irony of my situation—sitting in a quaint bar in Carmel, surrounded by the laughter of carefree tourists, while my insides twist into knots. Oh, the joys of living a life that isn't really yours. *Cheers, Kelly.*

So, here I am, swirling my wine and pretending to enjoy the solo jazz musician strumming away in the corner. It's almost peaceful. Almost. Until, out of the corner of my eye, I catch a glimpse of someone at the far end of the bar. Blonde hair, pale skin, that specific tilt of the head. It's her. It has to be.

My heart kicks against my chest like it's trying to break out. No, it can't be Kelly. She's supposed to be in a coma, tucked safely away in some sterile hospital room. But paranoia, like wine, only needs a little to get you going—a sip, a glimpse, and you're off to the races. I squint, trying to get a better look without seeming like I'm staring. The woman laughs, and it's like a punch to the gut. That laugh. I've heard it a thousand times across from me in sessions that were supposed to help me but ended up as part of my long con. The same laugh I heard before the hot coals marred her face, before the world flipped upside down. Before I left Kelly for dead.

Taking a long drink, I force a laugh of my own, high and a bit too shrill. Taylor gives me a sideways glance, probably wondering if I'm one sip away from a breakdown. *Honey, if only you knew.*

"Another glass, please," I say with a tilt of my almost-empty glass, my voice a tad steadier than I feel. He nods, and as he turns to fetch another carafe, I take the opportunity to scrutinize the woman more closely. But as I stare, the details don't line up. The woman's nose is wrong, her lips fuller. She catches me looking and offers a cautious smile—the polite, reserved kind you give to someone who's gawking at you. *God, Shae, get it together.*

I turn back to my freshly poured glass, chiding myself. Of course it's not Kelly. My brain knows this, but my guilty conscience? That's another story. It's running wild, crafting narratives where Kelly wakes from her coma, tracks me down, and confronts me in a dramatic showdown right here, amid unsuspecting winos. Taking a deep breath, I try to focus on the music, the real people around me, anything to anchor myself back to reality. But my mind is a traitor, looping back to that day—the sizzle of hot coals, her pained moans as heat blistered her cheeks, and finally, Kelly's body slumped over.

Panic claws its way up my throat, and my breaths come quick and shallow. Everyone must know. They must see the guilt written all over my face. I shift abruptly, my chair scraping loudly against the wooden floor. A few heads turn, a couple of frowns directed my way. Perfect, a scene. Just what I need. I turn to focus my gaze out the window, the quaint charm of the town mocking me with its tranquility. I imagine what the real Kelly might say if she bumped into me here.

"Healed and hunting for you, Shae," I mutter to myself, turning away from the woman and deeper into my personal labyrinth of paranoia.

Kelly's not here. She can't hurt me. But as I focus on the dimming light of Carmel out the windows, I realize that it doesn't matter. She's already haunting me, a specter crafted from my own deeds, following me into every shadow, every reflection, every glass of wine. And I can't escape her, not really.

"So, give me all the juicy details of your affair," Taylor returns.

"What?!" I choke out a laugh. "There is no affair—"

"Well, I might have been lying when I said I saw you on the porch."

"You didn't?" My brows knit together with confusion.

"Saw you in the back, on the balcony too."

"What?" I move to push myself off the barstool, embarrassed that my new neighbor really does seem to be watching my every move.

"Stop, stop. I just went out for a joint and saw you on the balcony making out. As soon as I saw you there, I left. Took my board and my joint down to the beach. I wasn't watching you like a creeper, Kelly."

I don't reply because I don't believe him.

"So, you didn't see us on the porch?"

"I did, on my walk back from the beach. Look, I really don't care. Love is love and whatever. I'm not into laws and labels and shit. As long as everyone's having fun—"

"Are you always this nosy?" I blurt.

He shrugs. "I'm a bartender. It's part of the job." His eyes hang on mine. "You're a tough nut. Who hurt you, Kelly?"

I have to suppress a groan. I hate that he keeps using that name. Why did I have to be a Kelly in this life? I don't feel like a Kelly, and every time he says the name, it makes my skin crawl.

"Nobody hurt me. Who hurt you?" I shoot back.

"Life. The world. The patriarchy. Take your pick." His laugh comes easily. That's one thing I do like about Taylor—he doesn't seem to take anything seriously. Like he's sailing through life without a care in the world. "So, you're the expert they hired to fix their marriage. But instead, you're—"

"I don't want to talk about work, thanks." I cut him off. "Do you surf at night often?" I'll need to be more mindful of Taylor's schedule now that I know he always seems to be paying attention to me.

"I surf whenever I can." His eyes narrow. "Where are you from? Originally, I mean."

"Santa Cruz," I say without a second thought. I plunge my teeth into my bottom lip just to prevent more details from tumbling out. Taylor is so easy to talk to, I forget all the lies I'm supposed to be spinning. With him, I almost feel like I can be myself, and I can't have that.

"Santa Cruz . . . nice area. You're not far from home, then," he muses.

"Where are you from?"

"Laguna Beach." He names a city just south of El Segundo. My mind falls back to the last place Dean and I lived—a cheap condo with a partial ocean view, all heaved cement and senior citizens on a fixed income. After living in Malibu and the Hollywood Hills, El Segundo was another version of hell.

"Laguna is a good town."

"It is." He nods as a couple comes in and sits at the opposite end of the bar from us. They cuddle up close, and the man slides a palm around the woman's neck and pulls her in for a passionate kiss.

"Whoa, they're a hot couple," I comment.

"They're here every night. I think they're having an affair."

I laugh. "Why?"

"No one is that hot and heavy without a touch of the forbidden."

"Hmm." I consider his words. "You're a pretty observant guy."

He shrugs. "It's a gift."

"Being nosy is a gift?" I tease.

He smiles. "So . . . what are you, thirty-two? Thirty-four? Where's your happily-ever-after? Just haven't found the right guy yet?"

The dark thought comes to my mind that I'm too busy stealing someone else's happily-ever-after to think about my own.

"Guess not. I'm too busy with work to do much dating," I explain.

"Is that so?" Taylor arches one eyebrow. "Well"—he grins—"if that changes, you let me know, Kelly Fraser, PhD."

A tight smile lifts my lips as anxiety chokes me. He must've read Kelly's name on the little business sign stuck in the ground in her front yard. Or maybe he saw it on the plastic cling with her logo that graces the door of her office. Either way, I can't stand that he knows Kelly's name—*my* name.

Taylor saunters off to the other end of the bar to take the couple's order. I let my thoughts linger on the fantasy of pivoting Isaac away from his cozy life and inserting myself seamlessly, just like I did with Kelly. Maybe my next journey is as a housewife and mom. Maybe I've been running from something that was waiting patiently for me all along.

An idea occurs to me then. I dig through my bag until I find a pen and a stack of sticky notes in the shape of sultry, pursed lips. I write out a quick note in my loopiest, most feminine handwriting. ***Missing you. xo*** is all I write, and then I tuck it into my bag to deposit at Isaac's house later for Brianna to find.

Isaac was mine once, even if just for a moment. I have faith that I can get him back. If anything, I'm more adept at getting my way now. My understanding of men in the years since we knew each other last has deepened.

Then, I was the prey in Isaac's game. But now, I am the predator.

CHAPTER 19

Shae doesn't seem to be in touch with reality, begins an entry in one of Kelly's notebooks. I roll my eyes, my stomach twisting into knots as I reread the line.

Shae doesn't seem to be in touch with reality.

It's not like Kelly would know reality if it bit her in the ass. The woman doesn't talk to her parents, doesn't talk to her sister, doesn't have any friends. She's insulated herself and lives only for her work. It's pathetic, made worse by the fact that her job didn't even provide her a decent-enough living for any of the finer things in life. In fact, based on the quantity of these notebooks, I'd say her entire world revolved around me. How's that for a reality? Surround yourself with crazy people, and don't forget to pass judgment on them.

She seems to have blocked out any signs of trauma or abuse in her past that I know exist in her earliest years. My only question is if she's blocked out the tragedies and is fully dissociated, or if she chose to for-get all of it. If she's still choosing. If she did choose to forget, then that makes her quite the accomplished liar. I've caught her in many lies over our years together, but that by itself isn't unusual. The brain has a way of twisting memories to fit our preferred narrative, and the more time passes, the more those memories can evolve. It's less the selective memories that are problematic and more the way she exhibits emotion—or the complete lack thereof.

I pause my reading for a moment to digest what Kelly has written about me.

Shae appears to use emotion to her advantage. She doesn't seem to feel things in the same arrangement others do. In fact, it almost seems as if she looks to me to measure my reaction before responding. She plays with feelings like well-planned chess maneuvers over an authentic expression of emotion. I've never met someone quite like her, and I'm honestly fascinated by the way her mind works. Was Shae born this way? I've tried to look for clues that might indicate she was born with some deficit of feeling, versus the more likely scenario—that life beat it out of her.

I don't know what to wish for. On the one hand, I want desperately for her to have been born this way. I've never treated a sociopath, and, professional or not, the idea of treating someone with such a disorder is intriguing, to say the least. Maybe it's the reason I've continued to treat her, out of my own curiosity over her health and well-being. It's not that I've done anything unethical, but most therapists would have refused to treat this woman long before now. She cancels at the last minute without explanation, and sometimes we go weeks or even months without contact. She refuses to do any of the homework or read any of the books I've suggested for her. She simply doesn't seem to want to get better.

But if that's the truth, then why does she continue to see me? Why bother if not for the desire to heal and grow? Sociopathy is often accompanied by narcissism. Does she simply like telling me her stories— whether they're fact or fiction? What I know for sure is that Shae is well-versed in lying. She has a scary good talent for it. But I keep asking myself—is a sociopath still a liar, or are their lies excused because they're diseased? Does a diagnosis change the ethical implications of her fictionalized reality? I'd desperately love to spend more time with her, at home, while she works, when she's navigating her marriage, but that feels like it could lead down a path that won't end well. I can't put my finger on it exactly, but Shae is hiding something from me, something big. We were taught in clinicals to trust our instincts, they're rarely wrong, so why is it my instinct is telling me that this woman is dangerous? On the outside, she's so pulled together and accomplished. She's beautiful and smart and charming, and the world is at her fingertips, so why does an inexplicable darkness hang over her psyche?

I slam the notebook closed, unwilling to read another line of her bullshit. This woman only saw the side of me I allowed her to see. She was a fool, a pawn for me to play with in times of boredom or when I needed a quick hit of validation. I could tell Kelly was enamored with me, the way her eyes lit up when I spoke about my past—the parts I chose to share, anyway.

Kelly was nothing more than a toy, and the way she was always available—at my beck and call, really—was a tool for me to use at my leisure. Sure, Dean would often hurl insults about my long-standing therapy appointments, but I never took them personally. He was a hypocrite, and he still is—they all are. Reading Kelly's client notebooks has only proven it. No wonder she came to me in Lake Tahoe after Dean's and Jesika's accidents. This woman was obsessed with me. If she could speak, she probably still would be. I crack a wry smile when I think about that. I wish now I'd only removed her tongue. It would be the least she deserved after how she's talked out of turn about me in these stupid notebooks.

Unable to help myself, I open the notebook again and flip to a random page in the back.

Shae is lying again. I know for a fact that much of what she said in our session today is false—maybe even everything.

I narrow my eyes as I consider her words. How could she be so sure I was lying? For the first time, I wonder if she and Dean were in communication. Maybe when we had a fight, he went to her and gave her the real story, leaving me with my watered-down version. I was always quick to accuse Dean of being abusive because *he was*, but if Kelly didn't believe me, what did she believe?

I've continued to press Shae on her earliest memories of childhood, but it seems she has none. She claims that it was happy for the most part, that being raised by a single father was uneventful, if not downright boring. But that can't be true. I know it isn't. I wish, not for the first time, that I'd begun treating Shae sooner—that we'd started our sessions when she was a young girl, before life added layers of trauma and defense mechanisms to her personality. Shae's emotions are buried so deeply, I knew from the moment she first sat down on my couch as a teen that she carried more baggage than most will ever accumulate in a lifetime.

I blink away the strong sense of shame welling up in me. Sure, I lied to this woman and she knew it, but how did she still manage to find compassion and patience to treat me? These entries have become difficult to read because the sheer generosity of Kelly Fraser is maddening. Does she have no respect for herself? No sense of self-preservation? Why did she so willingly allow me to manipulate her if she knew all along what this was? If she knew what I was? How could she sit there and listen to me babble on about bullshit, knowing most of it was a figment of my mind?

Because I entertained her, that's why. Because that's what I do best. I give people a show that they're too bland and insecure to give themselves. Most people play by the rules, spending their lives coloring inside the lines, but that's not me. The idea of life inside a box built with someone else's rules is enough to drive me to the edge of sanity. It's the fictional reality that I created for myself that turned my life around. Allowed me to become the accomplished woman she spoke of. I turned my lies into a brand, monetized my reality to the extent that thousands of people wished to live vicariously through. I made my own rules, became the ruler of my own realm, and then made others feel bad about the mundane lives they chose to live. And I could have carried on with the lucrative farce if not for Dean and his stupid philandering dick.

No, Kelly wasn't fascinated by my mental illness; she was enamored with me because I turned rotten lemons into the sweetest lemonade. I took my disease, as she called it, and made a life of it. What else was there to do? Spend years in therapy, crying on her couch before I went off to bag groceries at the local market or raise spoiled brats in suburbia like the other women I graduated with? No. I became something. I became someone, the kind of girl who makes headlines with every move she makes. The kind of girl who dupes everyone at her criminal trial and walks off into the sunset with a new life. I became the woman most are too afraid to be. I became whatever the hell I wanted, because of my upbringing, not in spite of it.

Fuck Alice. I became the Mad Hatter who ruled Wonderland.

CHAPTER 20

"Kelly!" Brianna approaches the bar at the country club, arms outstretched. I plaster on a fake smile and stand, embracing her quickly.

"It's so good to see you!" I mirror her effortless positivity as best I can. "How has your week been?"

"Oh, you know." She sighs, sits, then gestures to the bartender with a flick of her wrist. He arrives quickly and greets her by name. "Isaac and I order takeout from here all the time. It's one of our favorite spots. You should try it some night. It's so convenient to just be a quick walk away from home."

"It seems like everything is a quick walk from home around here," I comment.

"You're not wrong." She laughs. "It's one of the things we loved most about this neighborhood when we moved in. Now . . . Well, it all feels so small and oppressive. Everyone knows everyone else's business. Sometimes we talk about moving, but then, where would we go? Farther up the coast? Definitely not to the south. I wouldn't mind the mountains—Mount Shasta, maybe—but Isaac would go nuts being so far away from everything. Plus, it's just better if he's near a major airport for work."

"How long have you lived here?" I inquire.

"Since the summer we got married. My parents spoiled us with the down payment for this place for our wedding gift. Property values have tripled since then. We could sell now and buy a few properties somewhere cheaper, but then, we live in paradise . . . Who the hell wants to leave?"

I smile. Sip. Then wince when a man comes up behind Brianna and circles her in a warm hug. "Nice to see you. Where's that rogue husband of yours?"

"Work. Work. Work. You know how it goes."

"Do I." The man grins, then glances to me.

"Dave, this is my new neighbor, Kelly Fraser. She's a licensed therapist. Kelly, this is Dave Robson, owner of every single Chevron gas station along the Pacific Coast Highway from here to San Fran."

"Well, not *every* one. Brianna is exaggerating." He reaches out a hand to shake mine. I take it and appreciate the warmth and strength of his grip. This man is at least a decade older than me, and he looks at least two decades my senior with the snowy white beard and hair. He seems kind though. I like that.

"It's nice to meet you," I say politely, head down but eyes cast up to meet his.

"The pleasure is all mine. Tell me, what brings you to the neighborhood?" He's leaning close. Too close for my comfort, but I guess it's good to know if I'm ever in need of a date, I can come here and find wealthy old men like Dave to spoil me.

"Just needed a change of scenery." I look at my glass, indicating that I'm not interested in furthering this conversation.

Dave turns back to Brianna and smiles. "Well, tell that old man of yours he owes me eighteen holes."

"Will do," Brianna chirps.

Once Dave is out of earshot, Brianna breathes out, "He and my father go way back. Actually, Dave is the one who tipped off my father about our house before it even hit the market."

"Sounds like a good guy," I offer blandly.

Brianna shrugs. "His daughter and I went to Berkeley together. We were roommates for a while. She told me some crazy stories. Actually, she was kind of crazy herself—total party animal. If he only knew . . ." Her eyes sparkle, seemingly lost in the memories.

I chug the rest of my wine and tip it to the bartender to indicate I'd like more. It's taking everything in me to listen to her prattle on about all this useless shit. Isaac clearly did not marry her for the intelligent conversation. I'm not even sure how she got into Berkeley—her parents probably made a generous donation if I had to guess. In just the few hours we've spent together in sessions, I imagine I've had more in-depth conversations with Isaac than Brianna ever has. This woman seems to talk only about herself.

"Sounds like you were close."

"We were. I saw her in here a few years ago. She's a housewife in Connecticut now." Brianna rolls her eyes as if there is no worse fate. "Do you have family around here?"

I press my lips together, surprised that she's finally asking a question about me. "No. It's been just me for a long time now."

"Oh, I'm sorry," Brianna purrs with something that looks close to real emotion in her eyes. If she only knew the truth, she'd probably sing a different tune. Brianna has a dark side. In fact, the girl I knew in high school fit the diagnosis of a narcissist to a T. My blood begins to boil as I try to shove down the memories of that night. I squeeze my eyes closed, grit my teeth together a moment, and ball my fists at my sides before sighing and letting my gaze land on her sweet features again.

"So, how has everything between you and Isaac been this week?" I redirect the conversation to a safer topic.

"Oh. Well . . ." Brianna trails off as the bartender arrives and fills our wineglasses. "I . . . I found something. I'm probably making too much of it, but after the receipt from the wine bar I found in his truck, I'm just on edge."

"What did you find?" I ask.

Her face falls. "A note tucked under Isaac's windshield wiper."

"A note?" I sip my wine as my stomach somersaults with excitement.

"A note that said *Missing you.*"

My eyes widen. "Did you ask him about it?"

"No. No, definitely not. I'm afraid he'll think I'm crazy. Maybe the note was meant for a neighbor. I just . . . I don't even know when he'd have time to meet anyone. He's home working all day."

"People find time. Trust me." She winces at my harsh words, and I pretend to frown. "I'm sorry. I shouldn't be so direct. It's the wine," I offer with an awkward smile. "It's just . . . I've learned, in all my years of practicing, a thing or two about personality types, and even though I've only seen Isaac for a few solo sessions, I think I have a pretty good idea of who he is at the core."

Brianna's eyes hang on me with a look of cautious interest, so I continue. "Certain personality types are more prone to infidelity—the rake and the siren, the lover and the rebel—" Brianna looks confused. I've lost her. I sigh and start over. "Are you familiar with Freud or Jung?"

She shakes her head. Of course she isn't. I didn't expect her to be.

"To use Jungian terms a little more simply . . ." I gnaw on my bottom lip as if it's really an imposition that she's making me explain this. "Well, it's impossible to tame some men. No matter how hard you try and no matter how much they think they want to be tamed, it just doesn't work for long. They're addicted to the dopamine hits, the thrill of the chase. The male brain just isn't wired for commitment like a woman's is. If I had to bet, I'd say this isn't his first time violating your vows."

Brianna's eyes are wet. She swirls her wine in her glass and then drinks the rest of it in one swallow. "I . . . never thought we'd find ourselves here. I thought we were different. When we met, it just felt like a meeting of the minds, like we'd both met our match."

"It usually does feel that way in the early stages." I smile and sip. "Was there a lot of push and pull between you?"

She nods eagerly, as if I'm reading her mind. In a way, I suppose I am. I remember all the back-and-forth between them because I was there. I was the third wheel in their demented little high school love affair. My heart hammers as I think about finally getting the revenge on her that I deserve. I used to cry myself to sleep—willing the pain to end, bargaining with God to deliver me, waiting for karma to deal the final blow. But karma never came, and God never delivered anything to me but more pain. Until now. Now, I'm taking karma into my own hands.

"I still . . . I just can't bring myself to believe it." She shakes her head sadly.

"Would a confession give you some sort of closure? I can tell you, in situations like these, the more you know, the more the pain digs deep and won't let go."

She nods as if she understands. "Maybe we could go back to joint therapy sessions—"

"No, I find it best if both parties can focus on themselves and their own healing and growth for a while." I know I'm being glib, but I can't help it. I want this woman to hurt like she hurt me. "Have you considered a temporary separation? Absence always makes the heart grow fonder."

"I have been thinking about taking a few weeks in Mount Shasta or maybe visiting a friend in Baja just to give Isaac and me some breathing room." Brianna's frown deepens. She gestures for another glass of wine.

"That sounds like a good idea." I pause, giving her a moment before I drop the next bomb on her. "Brianna . . ." I take aim with my next sentence. "I wouldn't say anything if I didn't think it was important, but . . . Isaac alluded to being unfaithful at our last session." I sip, delighted when her face crumples and tears track down her perfect cheeks.

"I don't think I can sit here anymore." She heaves a few deep breaths and then clutches at her heart. I know my words have hit their mark. "I think I need some air." She stands, gathering her bag in a rush.

"Sure, honey. I'll pay the tab and be right out." I plant a palm on her shoulder, sending her my most maternal look of sympathy.

Brianna speeds out of the country club, and two minutes later, I'm signing the credit card receipt and following her out.

"I'm sorry. I shouldn't have said anything," I say when I reach her.

"No, don't be sorry. It's better that I know who he really is. It does me no good to lie to myself."

I nod sadly. "Want to walk the beach path home? Salt air is good for the soul."

She sniffs. Stands from the bench. Stumbles. I almost want to cry for this woman. Not because I feel bad for her, but because she's so pathetic. Brianna acts as if her entire identity is built around her marriage to Isaac. Maybe it is—maybe she was raised to be nothing more than this, a kept woman. Wealthy. College-educated. Useless. I've worked harder in the last week than this woman has worked in her entire life.

My resentment builds when she loops our arms together and leans on me to prevent herself from stumbling again. Not only did she have the audacity to ruin my life, but now I'm supposed to protect hers? *Sorry, sister, I'm not your savior.* I don't even think I have it in me to feel an ounce of empathy for this woman who has been handed everything on a silver platter.

Anxiety bubbles to life in my veins. My muscles begin to tense. My breathing grows shallow.

Brianna guides us along the side of the country club and away from the parking lot. The cliff path comes into view. She leans against a boulder, bending to slip her Prada flats off her feet. She wiggles her toes in the sand and then locks our hands and pulls me down the path with her. She's acting like we're little kids again, best friends off on an adventure.

She wasn't the same girl back then—I suppose none of us was, but the Brianna I remember was petty and spoiled. She spent all summer with her clique of cool girls, torturing the other kids on the wharf who had to work during the summer, stirring up rumors and gossip like it was her part-time job. Maybe that's just what sixteen was; I hardly remember because I was too busy working and taking care of Dad and Sophie to think about anything else.

That was why when Isaac came along and noticed me, my initial shock gave way to gratitude. And then obsession. His sparkling gaze comes to my mind's eye. The first time we kissed. The first time we held hands. The first time we walked side by side on the pier, practically announcing to everyone that we were together. I'd stolen the homecoming king from his queen, given him my virginity, and it made me feel powerful for the first time in my life. Our romance didn't even last the summer, and Brianna was a problem every step of the way. Her envy was palpable, the way she talked about me to her friends—like I was a villain stealing her prince—put a smile on my face. I felt more powerful when they talked about me, not less. *People are gonna talk about you anyway. Might as well give 'em something to say*, my dad used to tell me.

I bite down in an attempt to control the bubbling rage that's welling inside me, remembering the time Brianna told everyone I'd hooked up with the least popular boy in our class—everyone teased him that he must not have running water at his house because he always smelled. I don't know if that was the truth, only that everyone avoided sitting next to him in class because the odor was so strong.

Brianna did her best to ruin my life back then, but she could never do the kind of damage that'd already been done at home. Brianna's bullying was nothing compared to the constant criticism and abuse from my father. By the time I was old enough to go to school, I intuitively knew that his emotional well-being was on my shoulders. If dinner was ready when he arrived home from work, I might escape abuse. If Sophie was fed, clean, and happy, I might escape his ridicule. If I could fit extra food in my pockets so he could save his cash for whiskey, he might actually smile.

Whiskey and Sophie, that was the way to my father's heart.

I'm sitting cross-legged on my bed, the worn-out pages of my favorite book spread open in my lap, but the words blur together. It's hard to concentrate when the air feels thick with Dad's anger and the sharp scent of alcohol that always seems to cling to him these days. I hear his leaden footsteps thudding against the old wooden floor, each step a small earthquake shaking the fragile peace of my little room.

He's yelling again, his voice booming through the thin walls like thunder. "This place is a mess, Shae! Just like you left it. Just like your mother left us!" The words crash into me, sharp and jagged. I shrink smaller, trying to disappear into the bedspread that's dotted with cartoon flowers, bright and cheery, a stark contrast to the shadows that feel like they're closing in on me.

I squeeze the book tighter, the edges digging into my palms. It's supposed to be my escape, a portal to a world where adventures happen in grand castles and dark forests, where the heroes always win. But today, the magic feels too far away, drowned out by Dad's slurred accusations.

"Why can't you do anything right? Just like her, always messing things up. Never good enough, never . . ." His voice trails off into a mutter, but the damage is done. The words echo in my head, a loop that never seems to stop. I know I shouldn't listen, shouldn't let them burrow under my skin. But they do. They always do.

The door to my room creaks, and I tense up, gripping the book until my knuckles turn white. Dad's figure fills the doorway, his eyes too bright, too wild. He doesn't seem to see me at first, just stares into the room like he's lost.

"Shae, why did she leave us?" he asks, his voice suddenly quieter but laced with that familiar bitterness. "You ever think about that? Was it because of me . . . or was it you?"

I swallow hard, feeling the lump in my throat grow. "I don't know, Dad," I whisper, my voice barely a thread. It's the same conversation, the one that comes up more often than I can count, and it never ends well. I know he doesn't really want answers. He just wants to speak the hurt out loud, and I'm the only one here to listen.

He stumbles forward, catching himself on the frame of my door. "You must have done something, Shae. You must've." There's a pleading tone in his voice now, like he's desperate for me to confirm his darkest fears, to absolve him.

I shake my head, pressing back into my pillow, wishing it could swallow me whole. "I was just a little kid, Dad. I don't remember her."

"Yeah, convenient," he scoffs, and then his shadow retreats as he turns away, muttering to himself as he shuffles back down the hallway. I listen to the retreat of his footsteps, each one loosening the tight knot of fear in my chest.

Once I'm sure he's gone, I let out a breath and glance around my small room, my sanctuary and prison all at once. My eyes catch on the drawings taped to the wall—colorful, wild landscapes filled with dragons and warriors, scenes I've dreamed up, worlds where I'm brave and strong.

Slowly, I open my book again, trying to tune out the last of Dad's mutterings as they fade into the distance. The words start to make sense again, pulling me into their rhythm. Here in these pages, I can be a hero. Here, I can be everything he says I'm not. Here, I can escape, at least for a little while, until the next storm comes. And when it does, I'll be ready, armed with my own stories, my own truths, holding on until the day I can write my own ending.

My breaths stutter as I fall back into the heartache that I carried for all my childhood. Heartache was something Brianna never knew like I did. Sometimes the emptiness was so deep and unforgiving inside my chest, it felt like I might die of a broken heart. Until Isaac. Until he breathed meaning and purpose and love into my existence. His tenderness mended the ache for a while, until I realized Brianna would never stop until she had her man back.

Like a dog with a bone, Brianna violated my life in all the vicious ways she could imagine every day. So now, here I am, balancing the scales of justice after all this time.

I swipe a large rock with sharp edges from the path and tighten my fist around it as I follow her.

"I'm so glad you're here. It's so nice having someone my age to talk to in the neighborhood." Brianna's words come out sloppy. Happy. Carefree.

I hum my affirmative as my eyes bore a hole into the back of her skull. "Brianna?"

"Yeah?" she hums without turning.

"Thanks for meeting me here tonight," I breathe just as we turn a curve in the path, finally out of sight of the club. Ponderosa pines tower above our heads as sand and granite come together in a small ocean alcove. "I'm so glad we're neighbors. I think we're going to be great friends."

"Oh honey, I think so too." I smile sweetly as visions of her lifeless body swirl in my head. Brianna will pay one way or another. I won't sleep until I make sure of it.

CHAPTER 21

"What do you think your wife would say if you told her about your needs?" I flip a page in my notebook, pretending to give a shit that my newest client is making excuses for cheating on his wife.

"Needs? You think she cares about my needs? The only time she ever talks to me is to give me orders about yard work or paying some bill. I'm just a zombie with a paycheck for her."

"I'm sure she doesn't feel that way. If a conversation in person feels like too much, maybe sending her a text message explaining your feelings would be better. A lot of my clients find writing it out—"

"I don't think that's gonna make a damn bit of difference," he sighs.

"So, you'd rather just continue on this path?" I'm trying my best to hold in my frustration with him, but he's probably the most unbearable man I've ever met. Fred is only coming to counseling because his wife threatened a divorce if he didn't. And according to him, he does not want to give her half of his money, so here he is, sitting on my couch and disagreeing with everything I have to say.

"It is what it is, Doctor." Fred shrugs, checks a message on his phone, then stands. "We're good to cut this session short, right? And maybe instead of meeting weekly, we could get on an every-other-week schedule."

"Is that something your wife—"

"What she wants doesn't matter. Not about this. I'm too busy with work to sit here and talk bullshit with you every week. See you later, Doctor," Fred throws over his shoulder and then slams my office door.

"Well, then." I huff, close my notebook, and stand. "Another day, another asshole."

These married men are all the same, looking for the stability of a mommy with the sex drive of a whore. I've started thinking of all of them as little boys in the bodies of grown men. My agitation grows as I think how similar Isaac really is—predictable in his weakness for temptation. At the end of the day, it's this weakness that I'm using against him. He believes himself infallible, but no one is. Besides, I know Isaac better than anyone. Maybe even better than his wife, because I know darkness from the inside out. I recognize his flaws and embrace them anyway, and, in indulging his habits, I trap him in a way Brianna never could. It's not that Isaac and I share love like he and Brianna do; we share something deeper. I see his soul for *what it is*, not what I *want him to be*, like his wife. I'm not looking to change him. My goal is to know him in a real and pure way so I can use him to my greatest advantage.

But first, he must trust me.

I move up the stairs and into the primary bedroom in search of the morning sunlight. It's not yet noon, but the sun blazes hot, heating the bedroom like a greenhouse. My phone rattles to life on the nightstand. I send the unknown number to voicemail, then wait a moment as the screen indicates a caller is leaving a message. I wait a moment and then check the message. A chill freezes my veins when a voice rumbles, "Affliction will slay the wicked, and those who hate the righteous will be condemned. Evil resides within you. Someday you will burn in the fires of Hell."

I delete the voicemail with shaking hands. I recognize the biblical quote, praying with everything in me that someone has dialed the wrong number. Tears push behind my eyelids as I step out into the sunshine that soaks the balcony in an attempt to clear my head. My gaze falls instantly on Taylor. He's in his backyard, watering can in one hand and a joint in the other. As if he senses my gaze on him, his head tips up and his eyes meet mine.

"Mornin', neighbor!" he calls with a friendly wave.

I groan, realizing he has a clear view of my balcony and probably everything that Isaac and I did a few nights ago by moonlight.

I wave back to Taylor. He grins, sets the watering can on a nearby bench, then walks across the lawn to stand under my balcony.

"Can I interest you in a Bloody Mary?"

I chuckle as he looks up at me expectantly. "Sure."

I leave the balcony and head downstairs. By the time I'm outside, Taylor and I are meeting in the middle of the yard, he with a hand outstretched and offering me a Bloody Mary full of celery and pickles and olives.

"Your salad in a glass, Doctor." He grins.

I thank him and then take a long sip. "This is delicious."

"Best Bloodies in the neighborhood. I'm famous for 'em."

"You are?" I ask, surprised. "I didn't know you had other friends in the neighborhood."

He arches a quick eyebrow. "Well, I don't know if I would say friends exactly. They had a block party last fall, and I crashed it. Haven't seen a single one of them since. You know who I did see though?"

"Who?" I hum, sipping as I sit down on a bench that's flanked by potted flowers.

"You and the other half of that couple you've been seeing. Again."

"Oh." A chill of fear swallows me. Is there anything this guy doesn't see?

"You were walking together on the beach last night."

"What are you, a one-man neighborhood watch?" I tease, but my words ring with truth. I'm learning that Taylor is *always* watching. What else did he witness that he's not saying?

"You seem pretty close to both of them. You really offer a personalized service when it comes to the couples sessions, huh?" He's teasing me now, and I don't like it. "I'm sure you know what you're doing though."

"Yeah," I say, "I use a variety of techniques to get people to open up. A lot of people sit across from a therapist in an office, and all of their defensive mechanisms go up."

"I bet." He nods, puffs on his joint, then passes it to me.

I shake my head and utter a no thanks.

"It's your life, not mine. I'm just a stoner surfer. Would hate to see you get in over your head though."

"That ship has sailed." I chuckle, then swallow another gulp of my Bloody Mary.

"Is that so?" He pushes, as if I'm about to tell him something he already knows.

The vodka is already working its magic. My lips are loose, and something about the ease of being around Taylor makes me want to open up to him. "I've been treating my former high school boyfriend, and he doesn't know it's me."

Taylor's eyes widen. "Well, no shit."

I shrug. "It just . . . happened."

"Is that ethical?" he asks.

I shrug again. "Who knows."

Taylor laughs. "What the hell. It's all in good fun, right?" I only offer a sweet smile. His laugh deepens. "You're a surprise. I like you."

I swirl my drink as I consider the sticky arrangement I've found myself in. And now, I've just revealed more details to a stranger. I should do some damage control with Taylor, I realize, especially since he's my nearest neighbor and apparently always fucking watching. I deliver my next lie thoughtfully. "I would never do anything to jeopardize their marriage."

CHAPTER 22

"Brianna moved out."

"Come again?" I say, sure I've misheard.

"And all she sent is a fucking text message. She said she needs some time, whatever that fucking means." Isaac swipes a hand through his long hair as he flops down onto my couch.

"Okay . . . Did you guys have a disagreement or—"

"No. Nothing. She went out with a friend two nights ago, and apparently it went well because she never came home. Says she's staying with another friend while she thinks about everything. I don't know what the fuck she has to think about—her life is all morning brunches and afternoon tennis at the country club. I work fourteen-hour days, and all she can do is complain that I don't give her enough attention."

"She's working through a lot of her own stuff right now. Sometimes the only thing you can give people is space and grace."

"Breathing room. What bullshit. I could have used breathing room a dozen times in this marriage, but did I ever take it? Fuck no, because she would have flipped out on me. But when Brianna wants something? She'll do whatever it takes to get it."

"She just needs a little time to sort through her thoughts." I say it out loud as I think to myself that Isaac should be more worried.

His wife has just up and vanished, and here he is complaining like she's a spoiled housewife. She is that, of course, but if he really loved her, he would have concern etched on his face instead of irritation and anger. I wonder if he's ever been violent with her. He's so demanding and in control at all times, it seems like it might be a possibility.

"Thoughts about what? That woman is so spoiled, I don't think there's a thought in her pretty head. She's only texted me twice in the last two days. Twice. Who just up and leaves without any explanation?"

I shake my head, a false sense of pity on my features. "I think this might have been coming for a while. By the time a woman mentions issues in the marriage, her mind is often already made up about leaving."

"Leaving? You think she's left for good?"

"I-I don't know—"

"Well, you've been meeting with her every week for a month now. You should know her better than anyone at this point." His green eyes flicker with annoyance.

It's weird. I never would have thought Isaac would be so upset over a trial separation from his wife, based on the way his eyes and hands were crawling all over me the other night on the balcony. But then, Isaac is probably the kind of man that can't stand to lose. Ever the predator, when his prey manages to escape, he doesn't take it well. Almost like an insult to his skill or natural charms.

"I guess we needed the room anyway. I've been feeling suffocated these last few months. I thought it was me, then I thought it was us, but it was her. I know that now. She's been . . . weird." His eyes flick around my office as if in search of something. "Got anything to drink?"

"Oh, sure." I leap from my seat and head into the kitchen. "I have rye whiskey." I take the bottle from the shelf above the fridge—never pegged Kelly for a whiskey drinker, but I guess you never really know a person.

"Sounds perfect," he calls from across the hall.

I consider all the things I still don't know about Isaac. Firstly, how great his memory is. If I told him my real name was Shae, would that trigger a memory for him? Does he remember anything of our time together all those years ago? Or did he marry Brianna and forget the rest? A surge of jealousy spikes as errant thoughts wage war in my mind. What would happen even if I did manage to win this man from his wife? Do I even want Isaac, or is this just my ego competing for a man who's been out of my reach before now? Isaac definitely holds a space in my head as the one who got away.

I start to think that maybe I'm the one who needs some space to get my head clear on exactly what I want from this situation though. I pour two fingers of whiskey into two crystal tumblers, smiling as I realize for the first time in my life that I'm just living in the moment. I don't care to know the outcome or control the future of this. My only goal is to do what feels right at the time. After all, I couldn't have predicted running into Isaac and Brianna ever again. I couldn't have predicted working as a therapist. How could I possibly predict any sort of outcome to any of this?

By the time I cross the hallway, Isaac is standing, eyes trained out the window to the perfectly maintained cottages across the street. I come up behind him, passing him the tumbler with a tender smile. "I'm sorry things have been so rocky lately."

"It's fine." He sips from his glass once, swirls, then drains the rest of it in one go. "Life is hardly paradise. How could I expect marriage to be?"

"Tending to a relationship over a lifetime takes work."

He frowns. Even unhappy, he is breathtaking. The dark flicker of his green eyes, the sharp cut of his jaw, the ever-present golden stubble—this man has always played a starring role in my fantasies.

"All due respect, but I don't have time for more work. Brianna and I were always easy. I need easy. How am I supposed to focus on building a business when I'm catering to her needs and wants?" is his reply.

I don't say anything because I don't think he wants me to. Isaac is a man of few words and even fewer emotions, as far as I can gather. He likes life simple and straightforward, maybe even needs it. I would have thought Brianna would be perfect for him; there's not a single thing beneath the surface of her. We've had enough sessions that I know that much for sure. I return on silent steps to the kitchen and grab the whiskey, bringing it back with me into the office and refilling his glass with two more fingers of the amber liquid.

"Thanks." The rumble in his voice goes straight between my thighs. I shouldn't be turned on by my patient, but then, this isn't just a patient. It's Isaac. *My* Isaac.

"I'm glad you're here," he admits, eyes hanging heavy on mine.

My stomach turns cartwheels. His gaze is intense. I feel chained to him.

"Got any more clients this afternoon?" His irises are dark with innuendo.

I plunge my teeth into my bottom lip and shake my head with a soft gasp. "No."

Where a minute ago, he was frowning, now his smile has turned into a sexy lopsided grin that steals my breath in the span of a moment. Isaac is clearly the kind of man who gets whatever he wants, and he's about to get me.

"Good." One fingertip brushes my wrist. My nipples pucker painfully under my camisole, and he seems to notice because his gaze drops to my breasts before that roguish smile deepens. This man destroyed me once twenty years ago, and I'm about to volunteer for his brand of heartbreak again. I vow right then that whatever happens between us, I will not have regrets. No matter how this ends, it will be worth it to be here with him now.

He slides his palm up my forearm, dusting my inner elbow before continuing along the curve of my upper arm to land at the strap of my camisole.

His eyes flick to mine. "You have goose bumps."

"I like when you touch me," I admit.

He's looking at me with such intense heat, I feel like I'm standing on the edge of a volcano, flames licking my skin as exhilaration courses through me right before the free fall. Being with him like this feels like touching the heart of that volcano, knowing the burn will leave a lasting scar, and leaping headfirst anyway.

He smooths his palm along the curve of my neck before he tightens his grip and leans down, locking our lips in a languid kiss. My muscles turn to pools of molten lava as I sink into him. His body is hard, solid as a brick wall. My fingers, itching to feel his skin, slip under his T-shirt to travel his washboard abs. Anticipation throbs in my system when he groans softly, yanking on my bottom lip with his teeth.

"It made me hot as fuck when you were watching at the beach that day." His voice is gravelly with desire.

"I—" I start to explain that I wasn't watching, but he knows me, would recognize my lie instantly. He and I are the same—pretenders. Fitting in with the rest of them as the darkness that splits our souls cries for release. There are two types of people in this world, those who follow the pack and those who lead with bold, reckless abandon, refusing to leave their lives to chance. Souls like ours are made of grit and greed. When we set our minds to something, we get it.

And right now, Isaac has his sights set on me.

As if he can read my mind, he tightens his hold on my neck in a possessive gesture that makes my body sing. "Would you say you follow instructions well?"

My breaths stutter and stall. I don't have words. But I nod.

"Good," he husks. And I am lost to him. *Again.*

CHAPTER 23

"I'll be out of town next week for work. I have to cancel my next session." Isaac's lying naked next to me, our bodies twisted up together in Kelly's organic cotton sheets.

"Okay." I smile, my body still hot with the afterglow of his touch.

"Maybe I should have said that before we took our clothes off." He chuckles.

I don't answer him. I hardly have words to express how I'm feeling anyway. It feels like I've been waiting for exactly this moment for twenty years. I trace a triangle of tiny freckles arranged on his biceps and smile. I love knowing the details of his body and his mind, the things that he keeps secret from the rest of the world. Knowing him this intimately feels like a rare gift. A man like this can't be owned. How foolish of Brianna to think she could.

A smile lifts my lips as a stray thought flits through my mind.

"What?" he asks.

I glance up, finding his gaze hooked with mine, an indulgent smile on his lips. "I just realized I get to bill insurance for your session today, even though we spent more time naked than clothed."

"Billing my insurance for dick, what a great deal." He laughs.

"Two birds, one stone." I stick out my tongue playfully.

"What a shrewd businesswoman you are."

"And still, I'm not as bossy as you."

The playful glint in his eye pulls me in. "Being the boss is what I do best."

"It sure is." I slide my fingertips along the swell of his pectorals and then shimmy on top of him, straddling his waist before dropping my lips to his in another slow kiss.

I feel intoxicated, addicted, ruined by him already.

The loud buzzing of a phone notification rattles me out of my bubble. I lean over him, swiping my cell off the nightstand to find that it's not my phone that's vibrating with noise. "It's not mine."

Isaac digs his phone out of the pocket of his pants on the floor. "Not me either."

Ice water floods my veins when I realize exactly whose it is. I think of the other phone I have sitting in the darkest reaches of my nightstand drawer.

"Well, I should get going. I have an early morning flight to Tampa."

"Tampa?" I hum. "My favorite Tampa Bay restaurant is there—surf and turf with the best view. I'll send you the link so you can check it out."

He nods, lifting me off his body and then rising from the bed. He pulls his pants up his muscled thighs and then shrugs his T-shirt over his shoulders. I miss the warmth of his naked skin against mine already.

"I'll call you when I get back." He's already moving out the door.

"Wait!" I shoot out of bed, wrapping myself in the sheet. I go to him, pressing up on my tiptoes for one last kiss. "Have a good trip. Maybe when you get back, we can—"

"Sure. I have to get going. I've got to drop the dog off at Brianna's parents' house tonight and pack and shit." He's pushing his hand through his hair again. The calm, cold, measured businessman is back. *Wait.* Did he just say he's bringing the dog to Brianna's parents' house?

"How far away is that? I hope I didn't keep you."

He shakes his head. "Just this side of Monterey. Not far. I'll be there and back in less than an hour."

"Oh. Nice."

He forces a tight smile, eyes flicking around the room as if he'd rather jump out the window than be standing here in this awkward moment with me.

"We'll skip our next session, then, and keep the following week?"

"Sure," he backs out of my bedroom door, then pauses a moment, eyes hanging on something in the corner of the room. "Is that a camera?"

My eyes flick to the ceiling where a small mounted camera is installed right above the wall-mounted television.

"No—"

"Have you been recording us?" Anger twists his normally measured features.

"No—not at all—it's just a security camera." I stumble. "A single girl can never be too safe."

His eyes narrow as he considers my words. "In the bedroom?"

I swallow, because he's right, why would anyone have a security camera in the bedroom? In fact, why didn't I notice it before? Has someone been recording me this entire time?

Isaac stands there, waiting for my answer. I shrug, unsure of what else I can say. "It's not even recording—"

"Then why have it?" his question is clipped. A shiver vibrates through me. His accusatory tone reminds me of the threatening phone calls I've been getting—could it be him making them? I'm just not sure of anything anymore.

Isaac's frown deepens. "Are there cameras in your office too? Have you been recording everything all this time?"

I shake my head, words caught in my throat. His gaze flicks from my eyes back to the camera before he waves a dismissive hand my way and then retreats down the stairs without another word.

"Bye." I force a friendly smile, but inside, the fissure splitting my heart widens. I glance at the clock. It's been exactly one hour since he walked into my office, and already, he's walking out again.

I sigh once I hear the front door close, indicating that Isaac is gone.

I swipe the whiskey bottle from the nightstand and move out to the balcony. I send off a handful of texts, and then, with the sheet still wrapped around my shoulders, I sink into the chair and take a long chug of the whiskey. I give a quick glance around the backyard in search of Taylor's form, but it looks like I'm alone out here. I sink a little lower in the chair as my heart sinks a little lower in my chest.

Missing Isaac is tenfold anything I ever felt with Dean. Isaac is wrapped up in my psyche, a staple in so many of the most memorable stories of my teen years. A simple flip through my yearbook would prove his status as *that guy* to everyone at Santa Cruz High. Plus, Isaac knew me *before*. Before tragedy twisted my mind into a tornado of torment. Before up became down and wrong became right. From that moment on, connecting with people in a real way remained out of reach. My fear of the unknown and my bent and trauma-tainted brain felt lit with fire whenever the possibility of something deeper than surface level came up.

Isaac *knows* me. He is the only person I've ever let see inside my soul. Not Dean or Kelly or anyone else. Only *him*. Surely, I've left an imprint somewhere on his mind. I just have to trigger his memory in a familiar way without revealing my true identity.

We are meant to be. We always have been. I've long believed that love is a matter of timing more than anything else. And finally, the time is ours. Stealing Brianna's life out from under her has proven to be as easy as taking candy from a baby. She shouldn't leave her life so open to chance. After all, if you're not actively tending your garden, it's dying. At that moment, a seagull squawks and dive-bombs the balcony. I jump, a scream escaping from my lips at the pure surprise of it.

I think of the garden statue of a seagull in Isaac's front yard and smile. It's a sign from the universe.

In the next moment, my cell phone rattles to life with an incoming text notification. My mind swirls with anxious adrenaline as I try to keep the circumstances surrounding the current situation straight. I shoot a quick reply over text. It's then I realize that maybe someone has access to the security camera feed—maybe the same someone who's been shooting threatening messages my way. Anxiety chugs through my veins at the thought. I'm not sure how sustainable this life is—my sleep has already been affected from the anxiety of it all—but I need to keep calm and carry on.

It's the only choice I have.

CHAPTER 24

"A glass of wine, miss?" The bartender smiles.

"Yes, please." I send him a smile back and then adjust on my barstool, eyes traveling out to the golf course and the Pacific Ocean beyond. It's early, just after noon, and my muscles still ache with the sweet reminder of Isaac. I imagine running into him on the green sometime. A thought crosses my mind to book a golfing lesson or, better yet, ask one of the old guys here to teach me.

A group of four middle-aged men shuffles into the bar area. I smile warmly at the tallest in the group, and then when he moves aside, my heart drops. A broad expanse of shoulder, wavy brown hair with gray at the temples, and a thick waist that looks all too familiar are revealed. I know that shirt. A lime-green Lacoste golf shirt I bought him for his birthday one year.

It's Dean. I know it is.

Can he really be healthy enough to play golf? I thought for sure he'd be in a wheelchair for life. I frown, realizing how fucked I am if my husband recognizes me.

The bartender returns then, sliding a glass of red wine to me. "Starting a tab?"

I nod, unable to form a single word. When the bartender leaves, I'm left staring at my own reflection in the mirror behind the bar. I'm almost positive he wouldn't recognize me. Where before, my blonde hair was chopped into a wavy, shoulder-length bob, it's now nearly to my waist. My makeup was always soft and natural before, but now I wear a deep red Chanel rouge lipstick and bloodred nails all day, every day without fail. I've lost nearly seventy pounds since last he saw me—in court, when I was pretending to be pregnant.

I gulp down fear and then cast my gaze to the group of men in the mirror. The man who's the spitting image of Dean turns and catches my gaze. I breathe a sigh of relief when I realize it isn't Dean at all but a stranger. I'm safe. I tip my wineglass to my lips and empty it in one very long swallow before setting it on the bar. The bartender notices and arrives to refill me within seconds.

"Thank you," I whisper.

My thoughts sizzle with anxiety as I consider how close Dean really is. I should have known he'd never last in Chicago—it's too cold and windy. Dean is really an LA boy through and through. If anything, I assumed he'd move back there. Paranoia swirls with the wine in my system as I begin to imagine a reality where Dean is on to me and it's only a matter of time before I'm ambushed. Just like when I was with Kelly at the Ritz in Lake Tahoe.

The soft ripples of Lake Tahoe lapping against the shore provide a soothing backdrop as I sit beside Kelly on the wooden dock at the Ritz-Carlton. It's a picturesque scene straight out of a travel brochure—clear blue waters, majestic pines, and the distant mountains framing everything with their rugged peaks. Here, far from the chaos of everyday life, I can almost believe in the tranquility that Kelly embodies.

Kelly smiles as she watches a family of ducks paddle by, her expression filled with genuine delight. "Isn't this just perfect, Shae? It's so peaceful here. I'm really glad we did this."

I nod, my smile a practiced curve of my lips. "It is beautiful," I agree, because it's true, and because it's what she wants to hear. Kelly has always had this knack for finding beauty in the simple things, a quality I admire even as I find it naive.

As she turns to me, her eyes are full of that familiar warmth, the kind that has always drawn me to her. "I've really enjoyed our time together. It's nice to see you relaxed like this. You've come a long way since we first met."

I have, in a way, but not in the ways she thinks. Kelly met me when I was a tumultuous teenager, lost and angry, and she became the anchor I never knew I needed. Over the years, she's seen every version of me—or rather, every version I've presented to her. The real Shae, the one with sharp edges and darker thoughts, is a version I've never dared to show.

"You've helped me a lot, Kelly," I say, and I mean it. Her support has been a constant, predictable force in my life that I've manipulated when necessary and appreciated when convenient. It's a harsh truth, but truth, nonetheless.

Kelly's hand covers mine, her touch light and comforting. "You know, Shae, you're very strong. I've always admired how you handle challenges."

Strength. She sees strength where I see survival, and perhaps that's why I can't fully consider her a friend, not in the truest sense. She's too pure, too untainted by the harsher realities of life, or perhaps she's just chosen to overlook them. It's her weakness, this relentless optimism, and it's why she could never really know me.

As the sun begins to dip below the horizon, casting a golden glow over the lake, Kelly suggests a walk along the shore. I agree, following her as we make our way down the path. The crunch of gravel under our shoes is rhythmic, almost meditative.

"You know," she begins, her voice thoughtful, "I sometimes think about the early days of our sessions. You were so guarded, but even then, I knew there was so much depth to you, so much potential."

I laugh softly, a sound more bitter than I intend. "I was a mess, Kelly."

"You were just finding your way," she corrects gently. "We all are, aren't we?"

Perhaps she's right, but the path I've walked is one I've paved with half-truths and lies, a path she's never truly seen. The thought saddens me, a rare feeling when it comes to Kelly. There's a part of me that wishes I could show her everything, let her see the real Shae. But fear—that she would turn away in horror or disappointment—always holds me back.

As the evening settles in and the air grows cooler, I realize that this weekend, as lovely as it is, is just another scene in the long play of our relationship. Kelly, the nurturing almost-mother, and me, the perpetual project, always on the verge of being truly understood but never quite there.

"Thank you for coming to my rescue this weekend," I say as we head back, the sky streaked with pink and orange.

"Thank you, Shae, for sharing it with me," she replies, her voice as soft as the fading light. "You've always been so special to me. You know that, right?" She pats my hand gently, and I nod.

And as we walk back across the lawn of the Ritz, I wonder, not for the first time, what it would be like just to tell her everything. But some truths are too heavy for evenings like this, too heavy even for the broad shoulders of Lake Tahoe's serene shores.

I press my lips together, pulling my thoughts back to the present and digging through my brand-new Louis bag in search of my lipstick. I apply a thick layer of the matte shade as I try to keep my breathing measured. When I'm finished, I drop the lipstick tube in the bag just as my phone vibrates to life. The notification brightens the interior of my bag, and I pull out the phone. I ignore the message notification that lights up the screen and drop the phone back into my bag, turning back to my wineglass. I take a few long sips before I sense the presence of someone over my shoulder.

Glancing in the mirror, I find the reflection of Dave, Brianna and Isaac's friend from the last time we were here. I force a smile.

"Kelly!" He claps me on the shoulder. I suppress a shudder. "How are you?"

"Great! How are you, Dave?" I shift away awkwardly to gain some distance.

"Good, good. Been tryin' to track down Isaac for a game of eighteen, but—"

"He's in Tampa this week." I cut him off, hoping to end this conversation quickly.

"I figured he was busy. Never met a man with a stronger work ethic than that one. What's Brianna been up to? I usually see her getting her morning espresso, but she hasn't been in in a few days."

"She's good. I haven't talked to her much. I encouraged her to take some time for herself. Maybe she booked a resort up in the mountains. She's been going through it lately. I've expressed some concerns to Isaac about"— I lower my voice with my next words— "her mental health." I cultivate more empathy than I feel for the sake of this man. "Hopefully, she took my advice."

"Well, that must be it. She's lucky to have you, Doctor." He claps me on my shoulder again, and I cringe. "Well, I'll leave you alone.

Just wanted to say hello." His eyes flick down to my cleavage. "If you ever wanna share a bottle of wine, I'm your guy."

"I'm sure you are," I say before I can stop myself.

His eyes bounce merrily around my face before he waves silently and then heads to the group of middle-aged men who came in earlier. I hate him. He's the kind of man who thinks he knows everything and likes to talk about it. The more questions he asks, the bigger the risk he is. I'll have to do something about him. I know it.

I swirl, then sip my wine, eager to get my mind off Dean and Brianna. A thought pops into my head to *show* Isaac that he's on my mind. I grab the phone out of my bag, send a quick text, and then do a search for my favorite restaurant in Tampa. Isaac mentioned at our last session that he stays at the same hotel every time he's in Tampa because the steakhouse and the view of the bay are the best in the city. I open a separate tab and search Tampa steakhouses. A map populates, and I find that there are only two steakhouses on the water and just one in a boutique hotel with a view.

This must be his hotel.

I swipe through the menu of my favorite place in search of the salad I told him about, the chef's special—a Crab Louis made with fresh, local seafood. I rub my palms together, debating if I should really take this next step. I don't want to push him away by being clingy, but I do want him to know that he's on my mind. That I listen when he speaks. That I am more attentive, thoughtful, and giving than his wife. Deciding to run with it, I place the order for the salad and a bottle of their nicest smoked bourbon, and then I schedule the delivery at his hotel for later.

I set down my phone as a satisfied smile curls my lips. I'm one step closer to getting him back. I'm not sure if I'll fall for him or ruin him once he's mine. Maybe both. After what he did to me, he deserves to have his life burned to the ground, but I'm not feeling that petty.

Yet.

CHAPTER 25

Is this you? I wake to Isaac's text the next morning.

I blink away the sleep in my eyes as I take in a picture of a Crab Louis salad and a bottle of bourbon. A vague wine-hazy memory of placing the delivery order yesterday at the bar comes to me.

Yes, I type back. *Thought I'd treat you to my favorite dinner. Hope you enjoyed it. xo*

Didn't get in till late last night. It was great though. Thanks.

I frown, wondering what to say next. *It was my pleasure. I didn't sleep well last night. I've been having some issues with my ex. I had to escape him a few years ago, but I think I still have PTSD from the whole thing. Thinking about you in Tampa made me want to book a flight and get away for some of that salad and beach time.* I include a little airplane and a sun emoji just for fun.

I sit a few minutes, waiting for the blinking dots to indicate that Isaac is typing back, but they never come. He must be swamped with work, I tell myself. But still, his dismissal stings. Mentioning the fear I have of my ex worked like a charm on Bishop in Chicago, but I might have to rethink my tactic for Isaac. Because he is so strong and capable, I assumed he'd have a bit of a hero complex and come to my rescue with some words of emotional support or even a little anger at the man who hurt me. But nope, not Isaac. Mr. Calm, Cool, and Collected is giving me a downright chill.

I spend the next hour in front of the mirror, getting ready. Being this version of Kelly takes a lot more work than I'm used to. Perfect is the name of this game, and now that I've seen Brianna, my desire to be not her but *better* feels like a personal challenge every day.

After I apply the last swipe of red lipstick, I spend two hours working on my schedule for clients and submitting insurance claims. I spent hours on YouTube learning how to use the billing software before I realized that Kelly had switched her clients over to an automated billing company before moving to Carmel. Now, I only have to submit the client's name in an online portal, and the billing company handles the rest. It's a pricey add-on to her business, but her hourly rate is astronomical, so she can afford it.

My phone rattles to life with an incoming call. The caller ID is a local number, so I pick it up without thinking. "Hello?"

I'm greeted by the sound of heavy breathing.

"Hello?"

A soft growl fills my ears: "I know what you're doing."

My heart stutters and stalls. "Excuse me?"

But the line is already dead. My stomach twists into knots as I look at my screen. Maybe it was a wrong number. *Or maybe it wasn't.* Who could possibly know what I'm doing? And what exactly are they referring to? I've done a lot of things lately.

The caller's words run on repeat in my mind. *I know what you're doing.* I search for anything familiar in the voice, but there's a chance whoever called used a voice distorter. I run through a list of my most recent enemies, from Dean and Bishop to Isaac, Brianna, and Kelly. It could be anyone, I realize then.

My mind wanders to where Kelly is now. I've tried to search all I can about the facility she's in, but there are only so many pictures I can find online. I've been toying with the idea of visiting the facility. I know I'm playing with fire when it comes to this, but with the hospital only an hour's drive from here, I can't help the temptation.

By the time lunchtime arrives, I've already called the facility and arranged for a tour, claiming my mother's mental health is rapidly declining and I'm in search of new living arrangements for her. San Luis Psychiatric must be in demand. They aren't able to schedule me for a visit for another month. I spend a few minutes searing a salmon filet for my salad, and by the time I'm finished, a new text message is waiting for me.

Brianna isn't answering my texts. It's been a week since she left, and she won't tell me where she is. Am I really supposed to believe this is for the best?

I frown, considering how to answer Isaac. *There isn't a timeline for healing. Sometimes giving space is a love language.* He doesn't answer. I send another text. *If you keep messaging her, you might push her away further.* He still doesn't answer. I sigh, frustrated at how much effort I'm having to put into this man. *Would you take her back if she came home tomorrow?* I shoot my next question.

Yes. He answers instantly.

My heart tightens.

I hate him. I hate him. I hate him.

CHAPTER 26

Whatcha up to tonight?

Isaac's text message arrives a few nights later. I don't reply right away because I'm not sure what to say. This man is never just friendly for the sake of being friendly. He wants something, and I'm sure I know what it is. We haven't talked since the day after I ordered the Crab Louis and bourbon for him, and I'm feeling . . . Well, I'm not sure what I'm feeling exactly. Used, maybe. Taken for granted, certainly.

I let my thumbs hover over the screen before I type out a quick reply. *Watchin' a movie . . . with a friend.* I add at the last minute *What are you up to?* I'm not doing either of those things, but this way, he might think about who else I'm spending time with. In truth, I haven't made any friends here, not outside of Kelly's clients, anyway. And Taylor, if you could call him a friend. I'd rather not if I can help it.

Isaac's reply is instant. *Thinkin' it would be fun to have a repeat of the other night.*

My heart lurches at his mention of the crazy sex we had at our last session. I've been hoping for a repeat, but then, I've been hoping for a lot of things that Isaac isn't delivering on. I think about Brianna, trying to find a way to plant the idea that maybe this separation between them should be permanent. I have to tread carefully—Isaac is smart, far smarter than I originally gave him credit for.

As I'm considering what to reply, a new message from him lights up my screen. *Is your friend leaving soon?*

A smile overcomes my lips. It's nice to feel wanted. Dean and I fell into a friendship that evolved into something more, but it was never like this. Even in the early new-relationship phase, Dean never gave me butterflies or made me second-guess every thought in my head. I want Isaac so badly, I can taste it. I lose sleep thinking about ways to catch him and keep him. I drop everything when he messages and then ruminate for hours when he doesn't. I'm pathetic, I know, but I'm still playing chess. I'm five steps ahead of this man, and no matter how smart he thinks he is, I am the one who will prevail. I always do. And the fact remains that I still need to get closer. I need him to trust me more than his wife. Then I'll know I've won.

Movie just ended. I'm alone now, I reply with a smirk.

I'm coming over. Isaac's message is instant. It sends a thrill through me that he's hanging on my every word. I feel powerful. Seen. Desired. I'm drunk on the feelings only he elicits. I leap out of bed and hit the bathroom, brushing my teeth quickly before adjusting my night slip on my form. Just as I finish ruffling my hair and swiping on red lipstick, a knock echoes through the house. My heart squeezes. He's here. As I leave the bathroom, I hear his heavy footfalls on the stairs. My stomach twists. *Oh God.* I spent twenty years assuming I'd never see this man again, and now here he is, climbing my stairs after dark and making me ache because I want him so badly.

"Hi," I say as soon as he turns the corner and enters my room. He doesn't say anything, just holds my gaze with that disarming, crooked smile. He approaches, circles my body, and then groans softly before he has his palm wrapped at the back of my neck and is pulling me against him. Our lips connect, and from that moment on, I'm lost. He's in full control of me. Intimacy with Dean was bland, our bodies going through the motions of what was expected without ever fully connecting on anything beyond the physical. But Isaac has a way of crawling inside my soul and taking root like a bad weed. Thrill and terror chug through my veins when he gives me a look like he wants to eat me alive. And every cell of my body wants to be destroyed by him.

Isaac guides me to the bench that anchors the end of Kelly's bed, then slips his fingertips under the straps of my slip and lets it slide in silky ripples to the floor. He runs his palms around my bare back before he hooks a thumb in his workout shorts and shoves them down his thighs. His erection twitches with the cool air and makes my mouth water. Without thinking, I sit on the bench and begin to stroke him softly. He grows even harder with my touch, and I decide then that I want to make this night last. I take my time giving him all my attention, swirling my tongue and making a mess of him until his hips are rocking back and forth and soft groans are on his lips. I stop then, backing away with a teasing smile.

His eyes darken and he descends, cupping my ass cheeks in his hands and pulling me off the bench in one movement before settling himself back on it. He adjusts me on his lap so I'm facing away from him, and with my hands on his knees to steady myself, I run my heat along him in an effort to tease him a little more. He's having none of it though, because a swift second later, he's lifting me by my hips just enough to slide himself into me. I moan softly when he fills the length and width of me, his hips arching into me. He is frenzied, maybe even aggressive, and already, I'm addicted. I'll do whatever it takes to make sure we stay just like this. Just like we were back then, the first night we spent together. The night I lost my virginity to him. I've already laid the groundwork for their divorce. I can close this deal; I'm almost there.

"Mm, you're so sexy, Kelly."

And just like that, ice freezes my veins.

I gulp down a swell of anger, moving harder and faster against him as I focus on how good he feels. *I hate him. I hate him. I hate him*, I remind myself. *And I love him.* My tormented emotions crest, threatening to take me under. I jump off his lap then, reckless need charging through me as I move out to the balcony. He's on me, his hands cupping my ass cheeks before he grips my hips and pulls me against him. I hang on to the iron balcony as he pushes back inside me. Every thrust hits deep. His demands are brutal, and his hunger is insatiable. Is this how he is with everyone? Or is it just me he feels this desperate need to conquer? Does he recognize me on some instinctual level—our bodies meeting for the first time again?

I hate that he's called me Kelly in our most intimate moment. It occurs to me then that for as long as he is in my life, I'll be living this lie. Kelly's life makes me cringe, but I've made the best of things. I wear Kelly's life well—better than she did, I daresay.

His thrusting slows, deepens, grinds until he whispers that he's close. Moans of pleasure bleed into the air before he slides out at the last minute. I feel his hot release coat my ass cheeks. A dreamy smile covers my face before I turn and slip my arms around his waist.

He tenses, eyes averted to the moon above our heads.

"Do you want a drink?" I offer because I'm not sure what else to say.

"Yeah, sure," he replies, then walks back into my bedroom and across the space to the bathroom. He grabs a hand towel and then wipes his mess off me tenderly. His attention makes me feel warm and loved. When he's done, I step into my slip and then go downstairs. He follows me, hovering while I pour whiskey into a tumbler and then pass it to him.

He sips, pauses, then sips again and drops onto a barstool. "Brianna and I have been texting all night. She seems off. I'm getting worried. She said she might want to make the separation permanent."

"Oh," is all I offer.

"She would never get a divorce. We've talked about it—we said we could survive anything. Our marriage isn't like everyone else's. We . . . we've been doing life together for so long, I'm not sure how I could get along without her."

"I-I'm sure she's . . ." I struggle to find words. What's the right thing to say to a man who's worried about his wife while your body still carries the evidence of him inside it?

"I've already called her favorite resort in Mount Shasta. They said she never checked in." He's tense with frustration.

"Maybe she went somewhere new," I offer weakly.

"I can't imagine where. That's her favorite place. We spend every anniversary there."

"Well, maybe she needed some distance from all of the memories, somewhere she can just be herself."

"I'm about to start calling every resort within an hour of here. Her parents haven't heard from her—"

"She has a Zoom session scheduled with me in a few days. I can ask her—"

"Wait, she's still doing counseling?"

"Yes. She emailed a few days ago to schedule an appointment."

"She did?" He frowns. "Can I see the email?"

I shake my head. "I can't. Privacy laws."

His frown deepens before he takes another sip. Today, there's a different energy to him—a mix of excitement and confusion that's palpable.

"It's Brianna again," he says, a tentative smile playing at the corners of his lips as he glances down at what I'm assuming is a text message on his phone. He's like a boy on Christmas morning, eager yet unsure of the gift he's about to receive.

I nod, offering him a warm, encouraging smile. "It must be nice to hear from her so much," I say, my voice dripping with a feigned enthusiasm that masks the disdain simmering just below the surface. Brianna, always the elusive disruptor. What would he think if she just stayed at her retreat indefinitely, forever out of Isaac's life and mine?

Isaac's brow furrows slightly as he reads the latest message. "Yeah, it is nice to hear from her, but it's also . . . strange. She seems different. More flirty than usual, and she's vague about when she's coming back or even where she is exactly."

The therapist in me leans forward, intrigued despite myself. "How does that make you feel, Isaac? Her being so vague?"

He hesitates, his fingers tapping rhythmically against the phone. "I'm not sure. A part of me is thrilled to be getting this attention from her, but another part can't help but wonder why the sudden change."

Ah, there it is. The seed of doubt. I latch onto it, careful not to seem too eager. "People can sometimes act out of character when they're in a new environment. Maybe this retreat is giving her some new perspectives." *Or maybe it's showing her a new path that doesn't include returning,* I want to say but don't.

Isaac nods, considering this. "Maybe you're right. It's just that . . . I don't know, it feels like she's hiding something from me."

"Communication is key in any relationship," I say, my tone soothing. "Maybe when she's back, you can discuss these feelings with her."

"If she comes back . . ." He trails off, the words hanging between us like a delicate, unspoken truth.

I suppress the flicker of hope that dances through my heart. "Do you want her to come back?" I ask gently, a question that's as much for my own clarity as it is for his therapy.

Isaac looks up, his eyes meeting mine, and in them, I see a swirl of longing and uncertainty. "Of course . . ." he says, then his tone lowers. "I don't know," he admits, and it's the most honest I've heard him be in a long time.

I lean back, processing this, my mind racing with possibilities. What would Isaac do if Brianna didn't come back? What if Isaac finally saw the light—that he could have a more stable, supportive partner? Unprofessional, yes, but the thought of being that person for him isn't unappealing.

"We'll explore that uncertainty," I tell him, my voice a calm, measured timbre. "For now, let's focus on what you need in the present, regardless of Brianna's actions."

Isaac nods, seeming relieved by the redirection. We spend the next few minutes discussing his needs, his goals, the life he wants— potentially a life without Brianna. Each word completes more of a hopeful blueprint in my mind, one where perhaps, just maybe, I could fit more significantly.

"Maybe she's being extra flirty because it's her way of trying to rekindle something or spice things up a little."

"We don't need spicin' up, Doc. We never did. Fuck, I wish she'd just come home already. She says she misses me all the time, so why the fuck can't she just come home so we can get back to normal life?"

Anger sizzles to life as I realize what's going on here. He's using us against each other. He's using me, but I'm using him too. I'm using both of them.

"You're welcome to stay the night," I offer lamely.

Isaac doesn't reply. It's like he hasn't even heard me. He sips as if he's lost in thought. The silence hangs heavy in the room, and suddenly, all I want is to pour a drink for myself. I've only been keeping whiskey in the house because I know Isaac likes it. I've never been a brown liquor drinker, but damn if this man doesn't turn me into one.

"I've been thinking about quitting therapy." His sentence breaks the silence. "I think it's complicating the situation more than anything."

A shudder races through me.

As he leaves, I can't help but feel a twinge of anticipation mixed with guilt. It's a dangerous game, threading personal desires through professional duty. But as I watch him go, a part of me whispers, *Wouldn't I be better for him?* I sit there long after he's gone, pondering the blurred lines between duty and desire, between the life we lead and the life we want.

I'll have to do something about this.

CHAPTER 27

How are things going? I send the text to Isaac and then swirl the red wine in my glass. I'm sitting alone at the wine bar on Friday afternoon. Taylor isn't working today, so there's no one to distract me from my thoughts. I needed a change of scenery today, anything to get me out of the house and away from my lingering thoughts about what to do about Isaac admitting that he wants to quit therapy. We haven't spoken in the days since he said it. I can feel him pulling away, but it's too soon. I have to show him that I'm committed to supporting him, no matter what.

My phone buzzes with an incoming text. Expecting it to be Isaac, a smile curves my lips but falls as soon as I open the message.

I won't let you get away with this.

My fingers tremble as I reread the message. It's not the same number that called with the threatening message the other day. Fear crackles to life as I consider what this means. Someone knows something and I suddenly feel like I haven't done enough to cover my tracks. Who can I trust? Apparently, no one.

I consider replying, but what can I say? Whoever it is isn't going to tell me who they are, and anyway, replying at all just confirms who I am. Maybe if I don't answer, they'll think they have a wrong number. In fact, maybe they *do* have the wrong number. I push the anxiety from my mind, deleting the text message but not before saving the phone number in my notes app.

When ten minutes go by without a reply from Isaac, I finish the red wine and then send a quick text before opening the internet browser. The last tab open is a search for Kelly's hospital in Pismo Beach. I'm dying to know how she's doing. Has she made a full recovery? It's been two years since I left her on the grounds, face disfigured with hot coals and my freedom secured.

They say time heals all wounds, but not this one. The more time goes by, the more obsessed I grow with her. Maybe it's living among Kelly's things all day that has me unable to get space from our past. I feel like I've been living with a ghost, mementos of her life lingering in the vanity and the shower and the office. Even the car smells like her cheap perfume.

Impersonating my therapist has proven to be both easier and more difficult than I expected. Easy in the way that taking over someone's life—just slipping into the role as if they were never there at all—has been the easy part. It's keeping the psychological distance that's been tricky. I can't let the train go off the tracks again like I did in Chicago. I got too close, too soon. I wasn't measured or calculating, but that changed after the trial. From then on, I knew my future freedom was in my own hands.

It's always been this way—me fighting for my freedom. Sometimes literally, always psychologically. I'm pretty sure my mind has been in a state of fight-or-flight since I was born. I'm not able to shut down my racing mind like Sophie seemed so able to. I envied her then.

"Shae—" my sister lisps between tears. "When is it gonna end?"

She's referring to the shouting downstairs between my dad and his new girlfriend. But I can't help the dark thought that everyone in this house would be better off dead. At least us, anyway. Let my father carry on with his life without us to abuse. What would he do without someone to yell at and order around every day?

Without us, maybe his life would be more peaceful. He sure seems to think that. I'm not so sure though. I think he's the kind of man who kicks puppies just for fun. But still, I'd rather have him home, mad and yelling, than gone, left alone to contend with the unbearable quiet. At least when he's home, there's some sense that we are loved and cared for. There is no worse fate than being forgotten by someone who is your everything.

"Do you trust me, Sophie?" She's curled up with her favorite stuffed elephant on the floor of our closet. Our legs are tangled up together because our closet is small. There's a little camping light between us casting soft shadows over our faces.

Sophie's eyes are closed as she cuddles her elephant even closer. "I trust you the most."

She smiles, her eyes still closed, and I think now would be the time to do it. Suffocate her with that little stuffed animal. It would only take a few minutes. And Dad is carrying on so loudly downstairs, he wouldn't hear a thing. I'm sure of it. Maybe once she breathes her last breath, I can swallow the few pills that I stole from Dad's vanity. A murder-suicide, I think, just like on the crime shows Dad watches on TV.

Dead people always look so peaceful. I envy them. I imagine swallowing the pills and praying for my heart to stop as Sophie's lifeless body lies next to me on the floor. And then I think the whole operation would take too long. There's too much time for me to change my mind. If I'm gonna do this—save us both from the abuse—it'll have to be something quicker than poisoning and suffocation. It'll have to be something immediate and painless, something Sophie will never see coming.

"Shae?" Sophie says into the dim light.

"Yeah?" I reply.

"Will you sing the popcorn song? Daddy is yelling too loud. I can't fall asleep."

"Sure," I say, then begin the opening lines of the song she's been making me sing for years. I can't wait for the day I never have to sing this song again. Maybe I'll even forget it. Maybe I'll forget all of this. If I'm lucky, I can tuck these childhood memories in the basement of my mind, never to see the light of day again.

My heart thrums painfully as I think back on the night paramedics confirmed that my sister was dead—her last breath stolen from her. I didn't feel anything then. I still don't. I know I should, but the only thing I felt was a pressing sense of jealousy that she'd escaped and I was still there, getting along. Life was simpler but more painful in her absence. Nothing like I thought it would be. So, as the pain persisted, so did I.

A garbage truck emptying trash bins down the street shakes me from the thoughts running in my mind. I have work to do; I don't have time to think about what might've been.

I take a measured breath as my thumb lingers on the phone number to the facility where Kelly is. I have so many questions about her condition. What could it hurt using Kelly's credentials to just ask a few things? Before I can stop myself, I hit dial on the number. It rings once before a receptionist picks up. I ask to speak to one of the nurses, and I'm transferred to another line. I wait for a few moments while it rings. I'm just about to hang up when a nurse picks up the line. She sounds frustrated and overworked.

"Hi. I'm sorry to bother you. I'll make it quick. I'm calling on behalf of Shae Halston's family. I'm a licensed therapist and—"

"Oh, you people call all the time. It's like you think we don't have jobs or something. Shae Halston's condition hasn't changed."

"Yes, but the family was hoping she'd be well enough to communicate if—"

"Shae is unable to communicate. I told you, nothing has changed."

"So, she's still in a coma?"

"No, not a coma. Just unresponsive to stimulus."

"Oh," is all I can think to say.

"If anything changes, her doctor will give the family a call."

And then she hangs up.

"Thanks," I gripe. She's not communicating, so at least there's that. I've been wondering how this will play out. Will she ever talk again? Will she be able-bodied enough to walk again? I thought I'd left Dean for dead—at the bare minimum, paralyzed. But here he is, spending time in Sacramento, living his best life. I can't let that happen again. Dean's a wild card. I think briefly about taking a drive up to Sacramento to take care of him once and for all, but I don't have time to think about that on top of everything else. I have to focus on what's right in front of me, and right now, Isaac and Brianna and Kelly are taking all of my attention.

I hit redial on my cell, and when the receptionist of the hospital picks up, I ask only one question. "What time do visiting hours end today?"

"Seven p.m."

"Thanks." And then I hang up, gather my tote, and type the address of the hospital into my GPS.

A satisfied smile turns my face. I'll be face-to-face with Kelly inside the hour.

CHAPTER 28

WELCOME TO SAN LUIS PSYCHIATRIC HOSPITAL reads the sign at the entrance of the facility. I park in the visitors' parking lot, which is empty outside of a rusted red Chevy pickup. My heart stutters as I walk up the steps that lead to the imposing redbrick building. I'm suddenly rethinking everything. My confidence has waned in the forty-five minutes it's taken me to make this drive. I'm playing with fire, but how could I possibly get burned? Kelly has no family to speak of, except an expat sister who never checks in. There's no one here who would recognize her car or her name or anything else. I am safe. I suck in a breath as I open the double doors and get my first glimpse of Kelly's new home.

A long hallway with dozens of rooms on either side stretches in front of me. I move quickly, eyes scanning the rooms as I pass. I have to pause after every few doors to glance at the name on the door. I haven't seen a single nurse yet. It makes me think the quality of care Kelly is getting here isn't great. Poor thing. I think of the nursing shortage and the strike that allowed me to get away with disfiguring her enough to walk right out the door of the last facility, leaving her in my place. I'm angered that if I were her right now, I'd just be lying in a bed all day, waiting to be fed through a feeding tube. The health system in this country is so fucked up.

A nurse comes around the corner then, a file in one hand and a tray of medications in tiny paper cups in another. I smile easily, like I belong here. Her smile is tight when she passes me. I made sure to wear the lanyard with Kelly's badge hanging from my neck—it's the keycard she used to access the last hospital I was at—but I figure at first glance, it makes me look more official. Like I am one of them and not one of the patients they should be taking care of. I reach the end of the hallway and frown. Finding Kelly is going to be more difficult than I anticipated. I turn the corner, and my eyes land on a vacant nurses' station. I take a few steps closer and am surprised to find a list of patients in one column and room numbers in another. I scan the list quickly until I find the name I'm looking for.

Mine. Halston, Shae. Room 108.

I tuck my bag a little tighter under my arm and then backtrack, moving down the hallway that stretches opposite the one I just searched.

Room 102. Room 104. Room 106. *Room 108.*

This is it.

I hold tightly to my bag as if it will protect me like a shield if things go sideways in the next few minutes. I don't bother knocking. The door is already ajar, so I push it the rest of the way open. And then I nearly lose my breath. It's her. Hooked to machines that *beep* and *whoosh* as they deliver fluids into her system and track her vitals. I move closer, eager to get a better glimpse of her face. I let the door close softly behind me before advancing farther into the room.

When I come around the edge of the bed, I catch my first clear glimpse of her. She looks peaceful. Bloated by fluids and medicine. But peaceful. Which is a relief, because if she could see herself in a mirror, she'd probably lose it. She's obviously had skin grafts in an attempt to repair the damage the hot coals caused to her flesh. Shiny scars mar her fat cheeks. Bright pink lashings of skin decorate each dip and plane of her face like a road map. Kelly was never a beautiful woman, but now she looks like she narrowly survived an acid attack. She's so disfigured, practically beyond recognition. If it weren't for the name on the chart at the end of her bed—*my name*—I'd walk right by her without realizing we'd spent the last twenty years sitting across from each other week after week.

I expected to feel *something* being here and seeing her like this, but the truth is, I don't feel anything. I'm not mad or sad or guilt-ridden. I'm indifferent. *Better her than me* is all I keep thinking.

With my attention turned to the file at the end of her bed, I swipe it and flip through the contents quickly. *Shae Halston. 34. Uncommunicative due to lingual nerve damage.* I spend a few seconds reading through the stack of paperwork that details her most recent surgeries and medications list. Just as I reach the page that explains Kelly's physical therapy regimen, the door swings open and I'm standing face-to-face with the nurse I spoke to in the hallway earlier.

"Oh. I was going to push more pain meds into her IV, but I'll wait until you're finished with your visit." The nurse smiles, but it doesn't reach her eyes. She's backing out of the doorway before I can even think about what to reply. Her eyes glance down at the file in my hands, and then her face falls. "Has the doctor been in to discuss the update to her treatment plan?"

I stand frozen, brain surging with adrenaline as I consider what to say. "No, but it's okay. I know you're busy—"

"I'll make sure he gives you a call." She pulls a tiny notebook from the pocket of her scrubs and scribbles something down before tucking it back into her pocket. "I'll check back in a few."

And just like that, she's gone.

A surge of relief washes over me.

As the door closes behind her, I slip Kelly's file into my bag, glance once more at my former friend and therapist, and then walk out of San Luis Psychiatric Hospital with a new bounce in my step. Visiting Kelly was exhilarating and fruitful in a way I didn't expect. And since I'm unrecognizable and she is uncommunicative, I could actually be a part of Kelly's life again. The idea brings a smile to my face. Life is so good right now. I'm living Kelly's life to the fullest and doing a much better job of it than she did. Seeing Kelly today just reaffirms that it's better her than me in that bed. I can take Kelly Fraser, PhD, to new levels of success. I just needed old-Kelly to get out of her own way and let me take the wheel for a while.

Or forever.

CHAPTER 29

"I swear, nagging is her love language." Benjamin, my newest client, continues to berate his wife during our first session. He's been here for five minutes, and already I've tuned him out. He's just like the rest of them—regretting commitment, eager to break free of the marriage bond, and looking for any excuse to do it.

I sigh, scribbling the word *cheater* in big blocky letters in my notebook.

"How am I supposed to be turned on and actually *want* to go on dates with her when she just spends all of her free time nagging me about the kids and the house projects and the bills and—"

It takes everything in me to suppress another groan. I hate him. I hate all of them on some level. They're all the same—claiming they're different, claiming they're just not built for committed relationships, when in reality, they're just scared little boys afraid to grow up. I consider all the men I've loved before—all the men who have claimed to love me—and the waves of disappointment they inevitably bring to my life. Is it me? Is it them? Maybe it's both of us or timing or just human nature. The longer I do Kelly's job, the more I think we're all alike under the surface and our differences are only a matter of the protective shell we each put on to be accepted by society.

Benjamin's eyes flutter up and down my body then, heating my skin as they linger on the swell of cleavage under my soft pink sweater. Kelly's pearls are draped at my neck, and her biggest diamond, a two-carat teardrop-style that looks vintage—probably a family heirloom, if I had to guess—hangs loose on my finger. All of Kelly's jewelry is too big for me, and most of it is very traditional and decidedly *not* my style, but I'm making it work with some cheap plastic ring tighteners and a little tolerance.

"Are you married, Doctor?" A small smile pulls at his lips.

He's handsome. He's not my type, but I like the way his eyes twinkle with mischief when he checks me out.

Awareness sparks and sizzles in my veins. "I'm not."

"Have you ever been?" he asks.

"No," I answer.

His eyebrows rise with surprise. "Does that make you qualified to do marriage counseling?"

I force a tight smile. "You might be surprised."

He doesn't reply, but his eyes are still taking me in with that interested twinkle.

"So, why no marriage, Doctor? Just haven't found the right guy?"

I think back on my sad excuse of a marriage to Dean. We never connected, rarely had sex, and had fun even less. Dean and I were a marriage of convenience. We were good on paper for a while, until we weren't. Until he found himself fucking someone else.

"I haven't found anyone who's made me feel like it's worth it," I confess.

He nods. "I think we're more alike than different."

"Oh yeah?" My lips turn up in a flirty smile. If this man has the cheating gene like I think he does, I might as well use it to my advantage.

"It's pretty stuffy in here. Whaddya say we grab a drink at the bar around the corner? A drink helps me open up." I know his words carry more meaning than he's letting on, but I'm okay with that.

Ten minutes later, we're walking into Sparky's, a local dive bar that's only a few blocks from my cottage. Every surface is sticky with beer, and the smell of decades of cigarette smoke clings to the polished wood bar. It's more than a dive bar—it's the seedy side of Carmel. After-work locals in search of cheap beer occupy the barstools, and a few couples sit tucked away in cracked booths talking quietly. Benjamin guides us to an empty booth in the corner and then orders two beers on tap for us. I don't drink beer; in fact, I hate it because the smell reminds me of my father, but when in Rome, I think.

Thirty minutes pass quickly enough, with Benjamin four beers in and his entire life story laid out before me. I should start holding my therapy sessions here. Of course a man like Benjamin needs a little alcohol to grease his lips and get him talking. I haven't had to say much at all. Benjamin seems eager to tell me everything about himself outside of the confines of my office. And the more he drinks, the flirtier he gets.

By the time another hour has gone by, Benjamin is pretty drunk, and his hands are running up and down my bare thigh under the table. He's not my type—I'm not even really sure if I have a type—but I wouldn't imagine it's him with his thick, neatly trimmed beard and bald head. He's sexy, and the sweet way that he flirts is so different from anyone else I've ever spent time with. I'm beginning to think we'll hit it off pretty well, and if we don't, at least I'll be able to confirm my initial assumption that this man is a cheater. He's too good at women—too good at flirting—not to be.

He slips his hands under my sweater. His touch is tender, more than Isaac's. Benjamin is turning into the kind of guy that I would date—bad on paper but so intoxicating in real life. Isaac, on the other hand, is good on paper. He hits every mark for the kind of guy you'd bring home to Mom, but the more I know him again, the more I see him for the hardheaded, hyper-focused workaholic he is. I've been considering how long I'm going to spend living Kelly's life, seeing her patients, living in her home. Her life fits me, and maybe Isaac is just the kind of guy I need in my life to focus on my future and career.

By the time I'm finishing my fishbowl margarita, my head is thick with drunk adrenaline, and Benjamin's touch is feeling like everything I need right now. He doesn't feel right. I'm so accustomed to Isaac's aggressive orders and bossy arrogance, I've come to crave it. But Benjamin feels nice. I should like this. I should want this. It's not like I've met his wife. This is not a conflict of interest . . . *I don't think.*

"Ready to get out of here?"

"Mm-hmm," I hum, his fingers sliding higher up my thigh as he nods to the waitress for the check. Minutes later, we're stumbling out of the seediest dive bar in Carmel and down the sidewalk. We walk shoulder to shoulder, not quite touching, but just enough that I can feel him in every cell of my body. By the time we reach my house and we're behind closed doors, all of that changes. His hands are everywhere, his lips are on mine, and his palms work a worn path from my hips over my torso and right up to the dip in my neck. He's devouring me . . . tenderly. And nothing about it feels right.

"Stop . . . stop," I whisper.

He does, concern clouding his features. "Is everything okay?"

I nod, sniff, then let a single tear fall. "I'm just not ready. I'm sorry. My ex-boyfriend was . . . brutal," is all I can think to say.

He nods but doesn't say anything else.

One minute later, I'm standing alone in my kitchen, shaking.

I do the only thing I can think of.

Are you around? I wait a moment and then send another message. *Had a weird date, afraid he'll come back. Wanna come over for a while and distract me from a panic attack?*

I wait a long time for Isaac to answer. Longer than he's ever made me wait for his reply before. I wait all night. I manage to distract myself from the panic attack I was never really going to have to begin with by watching *Love Is Blind* episodes. I tuck myself into bed at midnight without any word from Isaac. I fall asleep thinking I'm losing him. That I'll have to change up my tactics to keep him hooked.

I wake up to a text from the man of the hour.

Thinking we should pump the brakes for a bit.

My heart stutters to a full stop. What does that mean—*pump the brakes?*

Pump the brakes on what? On us? On therapy? On late-night texts?

I wait, hoping he'll follow his message up with an explanation, but it never comes. By the time I'm stepping out of the shower, I know I'll have to reply something. I spend the next sixty minutes getting ready and formulating my reply to Isaac.

Pump the brakes with therapy or . . . ?

Isaac's reply is instant. *Everything.*

Everything? I cringe. This isn't going as I planned. I'd hoped for a few more weeks to fully hook Isaac on all things me, but just when we're supposed to get closer, he's pulling away.

Something is weird with Brianna. Her parents haven't heard from her at all. That's not like her. I'm worried, and I need to focus on that right now.

Tears burn behind my eyelids. Of course he's worried. I sigh, grinding my teeth as I think about what to say next. But I can't think about anything except how this man used me, *again*. Anger sizzles and sputters under my skin. *I hate him. I hate them all.* The way men use and discard women like trash is too much for me to take. That's why I wanted to prove that my hunch was right—Benjamin is that guy because they *all* are.

I don't reply to Isaac's message because all I am thinking is I want to keep him. And then I want to kill him.

CHAPTER 30

It's two days later when I see him again.

He's walking his dog down the street, and there's no way a conversation can be avoided because I'm sitting on the front porch. When he turns the curve of the cul-de-sac, I see his gaze fall on me. I smile as he walks closer and am surprised when he angles in my direction. He walks up my front path in slow, measured strides. With every step he takes, my heart hammers a little faster.

"Morning," I say as soon as he's close.

"Brianna texted me. She seems great, happy, lighthearted, and just . . . hopeful. It's like we're falling in love all over again." He thrusts his phone at me. "But look at this photo. It looks weird, right?"

I squint through the sunshine that's glaring off the screen. "She looks like she's having a good time."

"In Florida?" he spits.

"Florida?" I question. "She's in Florida?"

"Check out the sign in the background. It says Rosemary Beach."

"Oh." I lean closer. Just over Brianna's shoulder is what looks like a beach sign. I can't fully read it, but I can make out a large R-O-S in the first word.

"I think I should call the police." His voice is strained.

"What? Why?"

"Something isn't right. I can feel it. I've known Brianna since we were fourteen. Trust me when I say I know her better than she knows herself."

"Hmm." I suppress an eye roll. How well can you know someone, really?

"She's never even been to Rosemary Beach. Brianna is a West Coast girl. I'm telling you—"

"Healing is subjective." I interrupt him. "It can't be rushed, and it looks different for everyone. Sometimes a change of scenery is good for the soul—"

"Bullshit," he says under his breath. "It's been three fucking weeks." He drops down onto the top step. His dog settles between his feet, curling up on the pavement to wait patiently. "She's been in my life every single day since high school. How could she possibly think that just up and leaving me here is the way to fix our marriage?" He pushes a hand through his hair with a sigh. "I can't live without her."

His last words feel like fireworks going off in my chest. *I hate him. I hate him. I hate him.* How could he use me again, just to throw me away? All this time, he was just using me for cheap validation and quick orgasms. My heart stings. I put a palm to my chest and try to rub the pain away. I take a few deep breaths in an effort to control my emotions. My gaze lands on the side table, an empty bottle of Bordeaux and a corkscrew left from last night sit at arm's length. I flex my fist and imagine clutching the neck of the bottle as I hit Isaac with all my might. And then the vision of the sharp point of a corkscrew lodged in Isaac's throat comes to me.

So much blood.

I blink. Swallow. My fist twitches. I shove it under my thigh to quell the urge to plunge the corkscrew into his sun-kissed skin and reenact my dark fantasy.

"I need to do something." Isaac's voice shakes me from my delusion. "What do you think?"

"I think you should go with what feels right," I say absentmindedly, thoughts still lingering on the corkscrew. It's weird, loving someone and hating them in the span of a moment. Dean never inspired the strong swings of emotion in me that this man does. I can't put my finger on the reason. Dean did me dirty, leaving me for the tall, gorgeous blonde model we hired to represent my brand. Isaac's crimes are minor in comparison. I haven't even spent enough time with Isaac to know him, much less be this angry. And then I remember that night in high school—the last time we saw each other. The night he stole everything priceless and dear to me.

"I don't know what feels right anymore." Isaac's gaze shifts from me to the wine bottle and corkscrew sitting at my side. "Got any of that rye whiskey left?"

"Oh. Yeah. It's five o'clock somewhere, right?" I stand and head into the house. Isaac and his mutt follow me in. I feel his eyes on my back. My skin prickles with awareness as I pull the bottle and a glass down from the cupboard. I pour it and pass the glass to him, and he downs it in a single swallow. I watch with bated breath as he moves—the way his forearm flexes, the gentle tap of his toe on the tile floor. The way an errant golden-brown curl stands out from the rest. Without thinking, I reach out and stroke the lock between my fingers before I catch myself. An embarrassed smile turns my lips. His eyes hover on mine and do that twinkling thing that tells me he has one thing on his mind.

He doesn't say a word as he steps into my space. I inhale as the clean ocean scent of him envelops me. Just like a drug, I am hooked. His palm climbs the underside of my arm, grazing my shoulder before circling my neck and pulling me to him. My knees go weak. I feel trapped in a cage of my own making. From the moment I laid eyes on him again, my fate was sealed. Isaac's intensity demands my submission, makes me want to be someone I've never been before. He's my captor and my savior, and I wouldn't want it any other way. Isaac's attention is all-consuming; he lowers my walls and devours my insecurities with his need. After Dean, I imagined I'd find someone more tender and loving. Instead, I've found something I never expected. In Isaac's arms, I find myself. Like flying too close to the sun, Isaac leaves burns on my body that I won't soon forget. We share ourselves in a way that Dean and I never did. Let Dean have Jesika—maybe everything worked out just how it was meant to with him and her and me.

A dark grin slides over my lips then as I remember that she is dead. There is no Dean and Jesika anymore. I've made sure of that. It's easy to forget, when the criminal trial and psych ward feel a lifetime away from my life and goals now. *Correction:* Kelly's life and goals. I'm just borrowing the life she's built, trying it on for size for a while. Maybe I'll give it back to her someday.

Or maybe I won't. Only time will tell.

CHAPTER 31

"It's Taco Tuesday!" Taylor holds up a takeout bag in one hand as he climbs my steps.

I can't shake this guy. And even more surprising is the fact that I don't really want to. I know it isn't a good idea that I get close to anyone. Every relationship is a risk. Another threatening text message arrived in the middle of the night and I'm feeling on edge, to say the least. For the first time, I consider that Taylor might be the culprit. I've tried to remain guarded with him, but he's so friendly that he's not making it easy.

"Tacos," I finally say. "You know me so well." I laugh when he flops into the chair at my side and sets the bag of tacos on the table between us.

"Grabbed 'em at Moe's food truck. Best tacos inside the city limits." He reaches in and grabs one, unwrapping it and taking a bite.

"I can't imagine a better neighbor than you." I take a taco from the bag and unwrap it. "You're officially my new favorite person."

"You must be hurtin' for friends if I'm your favorite person," he quips, then crumples the paper his taco was wrapped in and grabs another. "Have you met many people since you moved in?"

I shake my head, taking a bite out of my fish taco to avoid answering.

"Didn't you grow up nearby though?" he asks, then chews.

I freeze. I don't recall telling him that. I never talk about my past, not to anyone. I don't even think Kelly knew I was from Santa Cruz, and she was my therapist for twenty years.

"No," I say between bites, suddenly famished.

His eyebrow twitches, but he doesn't say anything.

"Where did you move from, did you say?"

"I didn't say." I ball up my used wrapper and then dig in the bag for another taco. "I've lived a lot of places. Benefits of being self-employed and moving most of my clients to video sessions. I was thinking of going to the South of France for the summer." I throw out that last part just to divert the conversation from my past.

"Hmm." He finishes his second taco, then leans back in the chair and pats his stomach. He catches my gaze but doesn't say anything. It feels like he can see every dark secret shimmering in my eyes.

I avert my gaze from his. "Or maybe Portugal."

He huffs softly, then pulls a joint from a small case in the pocket of his cargo shorts. The smell of the weed takes me back to every summer job I'd had the misfortune of having on the wharf. I try to blink away a stubborn memory, but the pain is persistent, my thoughts falling back in time against my will.

"He's trouble, Shae. I can see it in his eyes."

"Stop. You're just jealous," I spit at my little sister.

"I'm not, I swear." Sophie's eyes are round with innocence. She's only three years younger than me, but the gap between thirteen and sixteen feels like a chasm too wide to cross most days. We've been fighting more since I started high school. Sophie has been attached at my hip since our mother left us, and I understand why—her absence in our lives

left a heart-shaped hole in my chest too—but I would be lying if I said Sophie's neediness doesn't get under my skin.

I find myself wishing more and more that our father was the kind of man who actually took his job as a role model seriously. If he'd only hang out with Sophie once in a while—watch one of her stupid movies with her or show up to one of her soccer games—maybe I could get some time off. But I've been raising Sophie since she was in diapers. Even before our mother split for God only knows where, the basic care of Sophie was in my hands. I couldn't bear to listen to her cry when they fought for hours on end.

Where were you tonight? You're cheating on me, aren't you? How much vodka have you had? Someday I'm going to leave and take the girls with me.

It took me years to forget the sound of my mother's voice as she hurled insults at my dad. My memories of my early years are sparse because I've worked to block them out. The burden of their abusive neglect was too big to carry—too enormous to understand. Leaving a baby crying in her crib with a dirty diaper and sour milk seemed unbearable to me, even as a kid. I couldn't understand how they could do it. But in hindsight, how could they hear her when they spent their evenings yelling so loudly, the neighbors often called the police because they were afraid someone was being murdered.

In retrospect, it was far worse. On my darkest days, I still envy Sophie's death—her ability to escape the pain permanently has always been my sole focus. And my father's drunken rages only escalated after the accident. He never spoke about her again. After her funeral, we carried on as if she'd never even existed. But I knew. I felt the absence of my sister acutely because now I was the only one left to take care of our father. It was up to me to make dinner, wash the dishes, clean the house, look after him when he stumbled in at midnight, too drunk to find his bed.

I hated him, but that wasn't new. What was new was hating Sophie. Hating her for leaving me with him. Hating her for making me take care of a grown man who had already inflicted so much pain. I hated my mother too, but she'd been gone for so long, I'd already hardened my heart with scar tissue to the loss of a mother I'd never really had in the first place.

"You're not going to like this, but I think Isaac just likes to chase—"

"Please, Soph, I don't want to hear any more. Isn't your shift about over anyway? I'll clean up for you, so you can get out of here a little early."

"I'm just trying to help. I know you were worried about his ex—"

"Sophie! Please!" I send my next verbal assault without even thinking about the pain it might cause. I am my father's daughter after all. "You're just jealous because I dated the hottest guy in school."

Hurt swims in my sister's eyes as she pauses, letting my words register for long moments. Her mouth opens and then closes. She bites down on her bottom lip as emotion brims in her eyes. I've never accused Sophie of anything, I've always tried to nurture her like the mother neither of us had, but I've had it with her opinions about my life.

Sophie wipes her eyes with the back of her hand, her face turning a bright shade of crimson as if I've just landed the final blow. "But, Shae, I heard him tell one of his friends—"

"Mind your own business, or I'll tell Dad you snuck out to that party the other night. I'll tell him you came home drunk and—"

"But I didn't!" She wails loudly enough that our manager at the ice cream shop sends a dirty look in our direction.

"I don't care. I'm not afraid to lie," I state coldly.

Sophie hiccups, unties her Norm's Ice Cream apron, and throws it at me. I'm about to hurl it back at her when a familiar shock of blond hair catches my eye. My heart clenches as Isaac and Brianna walk by the ice cream parlor window, holding hands and wearing matching tennis outfits as they head in the direction of the pier. A ball of pain forms in my throat as I realize, on some level, Sophie is right. Isaac just likes the chase—he's out of my league with his country club membership and summers spent on his father's yacht. I huff to myself as I realize the concept of a summer job is probably lost on him. In fact, the brief relationship we did have was probably just a way to pass the time. An interesting foray to the other side of the tracks with my low-rent upbringing and lifetime worth of trauma. People like me were born to serve people like him and his family, I finally admit to myself.

"Shae—" Sophie's voice is soft and pleading, but I stop her before she can say any more.

"Save it." I narrow my eyes in a warning glance. "I'll talk to you later."

She bends her head, tears still falling down her cheeks. "I just don't want to see you get hurt again."

I don't respond, only hardening my gaze. "Mind your business. You're just a kid."

Sophie clamps her lips together with unspoken anger. I know then I've hurt her. Sophie never gets angry. I know her better than myself because I raised her. She doesn't have the rage gene that our father has, and as much as I've tried to keep a handle on my temper, it still rears its head far more often than I'd like.

"I'll see you at home," I say, dismissing her.

She sniffs, then turns and leaves the ice cream parlor. I watch her form retreat into the summer night, her blonde waves swirling around her head like a halo.

If I'd known that was the last time I would ever see my sister, I'd like to think I would have done things differently. But even then, when it came to Isaac, I became someone else. Someone I didn't recognize. Someone I'm not proud of being.

"So, Portugal." Taylor interrupts my thoughts. "Would you need to apply for a therapist's license there, or can you really just do business anywhere?"

I open my mouth to answer, but then realize I don't know what to say. Why does it suddenly feel like I'm under a microscope with this guy? On top of the fact that he's always watching, I'm suddenly feeling like Taylor knows more about me than he's letting on. If Taylor is even his real name. Anxiety spikes in my bloodstream as I look for a weapon nearby to defend myself. Taylor might have brought tacos, but if it comes down to him or me, I'll always choose me.

"Did you say you lived in Vegas for a while?"

"Did I?" I tip my head, trying to keep my lies straight.

"Thought so." He lights the joint and takes a long draw before passing it my way.

I shake my head, top teeth sinking into my bottom lip as I think about all the ways this conversation could go wrong.

"I did for a while. And Chicago. And LA," I say softly.

"Quite the nomad. You're really livin' the dream, huh?"

"I don't know about that," I say. "But I'm doing my best."

"Where'd you get your doctorate?"

"Boston U," I snap as my annoyance grows.

"Great town." He puffs. "One of my favorites. I worked for a summer at the horse track." He grins at the memory. "Grooming horses, mucking stalls, under-the-table bets—all in a day's work."

"Sounds like an adventure," I comment, mind buzzing with ways to get rid of him.

"Are you from New England?" he asks.

"Mm-hmm," I hum.

"Or did you say Arkansas?"

My blood freezes. *Fuck.* Taylor seems more adept at keeping my lies straight than me. "Born in Arkansas. Told you I've lived in a lot of places."

"Were you a military brat? Or was your family runnin' from the law?" He chuckles.

"Something like that," I whisper.

"You sure are hard to figure out."

"I'm not sure why you'd want to." I stand, gathering our garbage. "I'm just a workaholic with a wine habit." I smile down at him.

"No. There's more to you beneath the surface. You're a weirdo—I can tell."

"A weirdo?" I chuckle.

He shrugs. "All the best people are."

I think how much I appreciate his friendship, even if he doesn't know who I really am. A smile quirks my lips because I think again how we're all just chameleons in life, trying our best to get along. I'm surprised to find that Taylor doesn't trigger me like most men. He's kind. Without an agenda. He is simply my neighbor, nothing more or less. I am relaxed with him, and that alone is dangerous. Loose lips and all that.

My cell phone dings with a notification. I glance down, frowning when I find that it's an automatic email notification. I unlock the screen and move to my inbox. My frown deepens when I open the email. It's a search engine alert for my name—my *real* name—Shae Halston. I click the link to the blog article, and my blood runs ice cold when I read the headline.

IT GIRL SHAE HALSTON WALKS FREE

I read the paragraph quickly, finding that some industrious true crime blogger called the hospital and, with a little digging, managed to discern that Kelly was released a few days ago—right after I visited her. I frown, wondering how I missed that. The nurses were so overworked and understaffed, the one I spoke to probably didn't even realize Kelly was up for release. But I pored over her health file front to back. It seems like it would have mentioned her pending release. Or maybe the doctor only approved her release after my visit.

Either way, this is a problem. A big problem.

My mind begins firing with options for my next move. If Kelly has been sent home, they must believe she's cogent enough to care for herself, right? Or . . . or maybe insurance is no longer covering her inpatient treatment. Less than a week ago, she was practically a vegetable in a hospital bed. Is she walking now? Talking? Able to tell someone what really happened that day at the old kiln at the last hospital? I have to find out.

"Everything okay?" Taylor interrupts my thoughts.

I let a soft groan escape my lips. "Just an issue with a patient." I hear the annoyance climb in my tone. "I might need to make a house call."

"Oh." Taylor swipes what's left of the bag of tacos. "Want a few tacos for the road?" He follows me into the house, trailing into my office after me. I hover over the desk in the corner, opening my laptop and then typing my name into the search engine. "Northwestern, huh?"

It takes a moment for me to register what he's said. "What?"

"I thought you said you got your doctorate at Boston U?"

"Oh. No." I clear my throat. "Sorry, I've been so distracted lately. I've taken on a few extra patients, and the onboarding process with this new billing program has been a nightmare."

Taylor hums, hovering at the doorway as his gaze crawls around my space as if he's looking for another clue that I am not who I claim to be.

"I need to call this patient back. I hate to kick you out, but . . . "

"Right, right. I'll drop a few tacos in the fridge on my way out. I can't eat all of these." Taylor's smile is tight. Like he doesn't believe me. I don't think I'd believe me either.

"Thanks, you're the best. I don't know what I would do without you."

He smiles, but it doesn't reach his eyes. "Sure, Kelly. Anytime."

By the time I hear the front door close, I'm aware of two things.

Taylor suspects me.

And I'm going to have to do something about it.

CHAPTER 32

A series of loud bangs interrupts my bath. I'm already two glasses of wine in, and now someone is knocking on the front door. I sink deeper into the steaming water until the repeated bangs tear me from my relaxed state. I spent all day searching for anything I could find about Kelly's whereabouts. Who could they possibly have released her to? She doesn't have friends or family; I made sure of that.

Bang. Bang. Bang.

"Ugh." I haul myself out of the tub and wrap up in a towel. Taking the steps two at a time, I'm dripping wet when I answer the door and find Isaac's intense gaze staring back at me.

"Hi," I greet him.

"Who are you?" he barks.

"Excuse me?"

He turns his phone screen to face me. "Kelly Fraser isn't a licensed therapist in the state of California. I did some looking around after our conversation the other night. Imagine my surprise when I did an internet search for 'Kelly Fraser therapist,' and I find this." Staring back at me is an old photo of Kelly, the same mugshot-style photo on her identification badge from the last psychiatric hospital I was at. "This isn't you."

"It is," I breathe, indignant. "It's a twenty-year-old photo."

"Bullshit." His accusation hits hard. "Tell me the truth, and maybe I won't call the police."

"For what? Forgetting to update my therapy license with the state? It just expired, and I've been in over my head with the move and this new billing system—"

Isaac snorts but doesn't reply. Instead, he pushes his way past me and into the house. "Prove it."

"Prove it, how?" I whisper, defeat loosening my muscles. I guess keeping up the ruse was never going to last forever.

"I don't know." He flops down onto the love seat in my office as if he's ready for our next therapy session. "Show me anything that proves you're not a liar. I'm trying to find a good explanation for this, but I'm coming up empty."

I frown, turning to look out the window. "I'm not really in a place to entertain this absurd notion you have about me. I went on sabbatical about a year ago and spent three months at a retreat in the desert. Yoga, juice fasts, hikes—all good for the soul *and* the waistline. I lost seventy pounds and gained a new lease on life by the time I came back. I don't look anything like that old headshot because I'm not that woman anymore." Isaac huffs at my explanation, eyes falling to his feet. "I think you've been stressed with Brianna gone."

"Yeah," he admits softly. A sigh escapes his lips before he continues. "Y'know, I was actually prepared to call the state and have your license revoked or report you for impersonating a therapist, but now that I'm here, that sounds fucking crazy." His eyes swim with frustration. "I'm losing my mind without her, Doc."

"That's understandable," I offer. "Listen, I know this has been brutal for you." I adjust the towel around me. "Brianna has sent me a few emails since she's been gone, and we've had one video session. She's fine, I promise. She just needs time."

"She emailed? I've been begging her to video-chat with me, but she won't. Can you show me?"

"No." I shake my head. "The state of California wouldn't like that. They'd probably revoke my license."

"Maybe if you had a license to revoke," he quips.

I frown. "It doesn't feel ethical to betray her confidence, but I know what a struggle this has been for you." Isaac waits for me to continue, eyes hovering on mine. "How about you give me a few minutes to get dressed, and I'll print out the emails for you and bring them down to your place?"

He presses his lips together in thought. "Fine."

I walk with him to the front door as my brain buzzes with anxiety. I'm not sure what I'm going to bring him, but now that I've told him I will, I have to come up with something. After the door closes, I rush to my laptop and open a new file and consider what to say in the fake email from Brianna. I sigh, realizing I'll have to find a way to copy and paste the headers that contain the date and time stamps. As if I don't have enough things to handle right now.

I sigh, glancing at the photo of Sophie and me that sits on my desk. My most prized possession and the only memento I've carried through life. She is my reason for everything. Having this image of us together, our happy smiles shining brightly out at me every day, has anchored me to my purpose even in my darkest moments. Juggling my new reality hasn't been easy, and Isaac is only getting antsier that his wife has been out of touch. I frown, thinking about all the text messages that have passed between them. He's desperate for her return; there's no doubt about that. If I were her, I wouldn't be very eager to get back to this man either. He's bossy and demanding and self-centered. It's exciting now, but after a decade of marriage, I imagine that energy gets old.

Truth be told, Isaac has always been this way. In fact, life only seems to have distilled his core personality traits even more. He's become so focused on himself that he's unable to even empathize with his wife's feelings. In fact, if anything has stood out throughout this process, it's that he seems dismissive and condescending when it comes to her feelings.

I stand from the desk and close my laptop, giving up on this path as my mind whirs with possibilities. I am stuck. My network of lies has ensnared me, and untangling myself from this web is starting to seem impossible. I am out of options.

I climb the stairs, and my anxiety elevates with each step. By the time I reach the closet, I know what I need to do. I pull on a summer dress as a heaviness settles over me. I don't know where I expected this train to stop, but I didn't imagine it would be here. I pull one of Kelly's dowdy knit cardigans over my shoulders to stave off the chill in the air. As I descend the stairs with slow steps, the cloud that clings to me is only weighing heavier. I reach the kitchen and pull the bottle of whiskey from the cupboard. I frown, swirling the amber liquid in the bottle. I didn't want it to come to this, but I'm all out of options.

I tuck the bottle under my arm, glance around the kitchen one last time, and then slip into my Birkenstocks to leave for Isaac's house.

I don't know what I'm going to do when I get there. All I can hope is that Isaac doesn't suspect me any more than he already does. I've done my best to gaslight him into thinking his concerns about me and my license are just his anxiety, but when I show up without the emails I promised, things are going to fall apart quickly.

Five minutes later, I'm ascending the front steps of Isaac's house. His dog barks wildly, always on alert. Before I can even knock, Isaac swings the door wide and greets me with only a flash of a smile.

I thrust the whiskey bottle at him. "I brought libations."

He nods, sauntering into the kitchen. I trail behind him awkwardly and watch as he pulls a whiskey glass down from the shelf. He takes the bottle from me and pours generously.

"Bring the emails?" he asks before he sips.

"My printer is out of ink. I can show you on my phone, but I'm telling you—there isn't much there. Just quick check-ins, like the text messages she's been sending you."

He grunts, finishes his whiskey, then pours himself another. "I'd still like to see them."

I nod with understanding. I settle on a barstool, my gaze taking in his space. The kitchen is quaint but modern, with unusual art pieces decorating the walls. Fancy bottles of olive oil and vinegar have a home on the counter. It would seem that Isaac and Brianna love to cook—or maybe it's just her. Perhaps that's why he's missing her, because she caters to him while he works all day.

"Thanks for coming down here at the last minute. And for the libations." He tips his glass and drinks. Anxiety speeds my heart rate and twists my insides as I wait for what's coming. "So . . . you got 'em?"

I clear my throat, pulling my phone out of my bag. I spend a minute fumbling just to buy time. I take a deep breath in an effort to calm my nerves. He arches an eyebrow in question. I force a tight smile. "I'm searching."

He settles on the barstool at my side. I can smell the whiskey on his breath. I think how ironic it is that after everything, whiskey will be the scent that will bring me back to this moment for the rest of my life. Just like the scent of damp evergreens clinging to the air sends me reeling back to the worst night of my life.

I spend another minute pretending to search my inbox for Brianna's messages. "I—I can't find them."

"What? Why?" He asks, his already-low patience running on empty.

"Maybe I have to be on your Wi-Fi to access my work emails."

"Is that so?" He sways a moment, the whiskey already doing its job.

"I'm sorry," I breathe.

"I can give you the password," comes his offer.

"No—it's not worth the trouble," I say quickly.

Isaac finishes his glass and then stands to deposit it in the sink. I watch carefully. His normally measured steps are gone. Instead, his gait is loose, almost sloppy. He comes back to the barstool at my side and sways as he settles down.

"You know what I think?" His words are slow, his cadence nearly a mumble.

"Hmm?" I scroll through my inbox, feigning distraction.

"I think . . ." He turns to face me, glazed eyes meeting mine. "I think you're a fucking liar, Doc."

CHAPTER 33

On instinct, I dart my eyes around the space in search of anything to defend myself. I gulp as he swallows up the air between us. The whiskey on his breath makes my stomach churn. My muscles tense and bunch under his scrutiny.

"Tell me the truth. Now," he hisses.

I gnaw on my bottom lip. "I—I—"

He grits his teeth, his patience on a razor-thin edge. "Stop with the bullshit. Tell me where she really is."

"You're drunk." I rise from my seat on the barstool, attempting to stay calm, cool, and collected.

"Fuck you." He leans into me, one palm latching onto my elbow.

"Don't touch me." My anger evaporates into fear.

"Tell me—"

"Stop. You're hurting me," I gasp as tears well in my eyes. He hauls me closer, forcing my body into his. I want to cry out, to hit him with something. Anything. He's powerful, quick, and far more aware than I gave him credit for.

"I should report you to the police—"

"And I should report you for assault," I snarl. His eyes flicker with a moment of awareness before he releases my arm and turns away from me.

I do my best to control the tremors that threaten to overtake my body. My eyes land on the only object within reach. The whiskey bottle. Moving swiftly, I grasp the neck and then, in the next beat, pull back and land a blow to Isaac's skull. The thud of the glass meeting his flesh is a sound I'll never forget. He doesn't even have a chance to react, his body slumping against the kitchen island before he falls to the floor. His strong, virile form has been reduced to a bloody, crumpled mess on the designer tile.

Isaac's dog whines, his alert eyes on his owner before he takes a few steps closer and sniffs at the blood pooling in Isaac's golden hair.

"Well, guess we have to do something about this," I say to the dog. "Can't believe how quickly the Rohypnol gets to work—worth its weight in gold, I guess." I think of the teenager I scored the date-rape drug from last week when I walked home from the wine bar. I figured it might come in handy at some point, but never in a million years did I imagine I'd need to use it on Isaac. A flashback enters my mind of our last date in high school. I think of the cocky way he told me it wasn't going to work between us—that he still loved Brianna, even after everything.

I hate him. I've hated him since that day when I was sixteen, and my hatred grew to intense loathing when I fully realized the events he'd set into motion on the worst night of my life. High school is brutal, they say, but knowing that still can't prepare you for the darkest depths of hell that run through those hallways. Especially when someone ends up dead.

I dig through my bag in search of the zip ties I tucked inside before I left the cottage. I find them and make quick work of locking

Isaac's wrists together in front of him before I pull and yank him with every ounce of strength I have in the direction of the doorway off the kitchen. When I reach it, I swing it wide to find just what I'm looking for—the basement.

I narrow my eyes as I consider the best way to get him down the stairs safely.

A low groan rumbles through Isaac's lips then, reminding me that I need to work quickly before he's conscious.

I'm not sure what my plan is exactly, but I'm here now, and the only thing I can do is make the best of the situation I've found myself in.

A moan falls off his lips and sends a shudder of fear through me. I underdosed him with Rohypnol—or at least, I tried to. It's not like I want him dead; I just need him to be incapacitated long enough for me to figure out my next move.

I clasp both of his zip-tied wrists, and with all my might, I begin hauling him down the stairs as gently as I can. I do my best to keep his head from hitting each step, but the rest of him is bumped and jostled in a way that I'm sure will leave bruises in the morning. It's funny. He's so in command of his business and health and fitness, yet now here he is, taken down with a low-dose tranquilizer and held by a single zip tie. And me. I smirk, thinking that no matter how much we plan for the worst, it only takes the span of a moment to have it all taken from you.

He groans then. I don't say anything, just continue to yank and jostle him down each step until, finally, we reach the bottom.

I sigh, wipe my forehead, and then plop my ass down on the bottom step to take him in. Even helpless, he is beautiful. The finely chiseled features of his face lend him a boyish look that's always cap-tivated me—and even more so now that he looks like he's fallen into a gentle sleep. My sleeping beauty, I chuckle to myself. Holding this control over the most powerful man I've ever known is intoxicating.

"What the fuck," he garbles, wrenching against the ties that bind him. He winces once he realizes there will be no escaping me.

"How the tables have turned, hey, boss?"

He blinks away the haze, his gaze finally focusing on mine. "Let me go."

"No can do." I smile.

"Why?" The word comes out feral, like the growl of a caged animal.

"Revenge, I guess."

"Revenge?" He shakes his head as confusion registers on his features.

"Still don't remember me, do you?" His eyes hang on mine, as if begging for more information as he tries to connect the dots about why he is here now, tied up in his own basement with me hovering over him. "The last time I saw you, we were sixteen."

His eyes narrow as he focuses his anger on me. "You're insane."

I laugh. "You're not wrong. And insulting your captor isn't the best tactic to secure your freedom."

He opens his mouth as if to say something else but then thinks better of it. His next question comes out calm and measured. "Who are you?"

I narrow my eyes, heart beating to life at the prospect of revealing the truth to him. I press my lips together, considering how much to say. "Shae."

His eyes widen. Narrow. Blink. *Shae.*

Long, silent moments hang between us. I remain still on the bottom step, my gaze boring a hole into his gorgeous green eyes.

"Why are you doing this?"

I shrug. "I'm an opportunist. We're really not all that different, you and I."

Isaac flinches, twists at his bound wrists, then his body goes slack with defeat. New awareness seems to light inside him as renewed anger bubbles to life. "Where is she?"

"I don't know. I don't care," I state.

"Did you hurt her?" he whispers. I only shrug. "What do you want from me?"

I shrug again. "To listen, I guess. To hurt you like you hurt me, maybe."

"How did I fucking hurt you? I don't even remember you."

And there it is. The worst five words that could have left his mouth. I lick my lips, allowing my mind to fully process his admission. My heart cleaves with pain. My first love, the first boy I ever kissed, the man who ruined my life and haunts my nightmares, has no memory of my existence.

"Well, this is why we're here, then. Because you took everything from me, and you don't even remember." I kick at his biceps. He doesn't even register that I've done it. He's so unfeeling, so lacking in emotion. How is it that I'm the one who's been diagnosed as a narcissistic sociopath, when the man who ruined my life and took everything good from me—including my sister and my will to live another day—feels nothing and remembers none of the trauma he forced me to endure? Where would I be without his destructive presence in my life? I wonder, not for the first time, if one thing had been different then, would everything be different now?

I shove the question from my head because it doesn't matter. We're here now, and Isaac will finally deal with the consequences he's escaped all these years. "I'm a big believer in karma, and for the last twenty years, you've escaped yours. There's no more escaping for you. Sorry, Isaac.

"You used me, just like you use everyone." My eyes sparkle as a dark thought splinters my mind. I know how to make this right. "You pretend to have it all together—the perfect wife, the brilliant businessman, the strength of a Marvel *fucking* superhero, but really, you're just a pathetic little boy desperate for validation. Brianna was never smart enough to see through your act, but I am. I've always known who you really are. It's funny. It's like the universe brought us together to deliver the karma you've spent your life running from."

"What the fuck are you talking about?" His peridot eyes simmer with rage.

My face contorts with heartache as my memory slides back to that night.

The scent of fresh rain on evergreens. A foggy shore and a deserted pier. Whitecaps licking wood pilings.

Sirens. Bruises. Blood.

"What is happening?" I ask the officer.

"A jumper. A tourist found her body."

"Her?" I whisper.

"A teenager. Poor thing." He grunts. "Can't let you go down there, kid. Isn't it past your bedtime anyway?"

"I just got off work," I say, tears sliding down my cheeks.

The officer glances down to my uniform, the Norm's Ice Cream logo printed on the top right corner of my shirt. "Hey, the dead girl worked at Norm's too. Maybe you know her."

I shake my head, but I can't form words. I know who the jumper is, and I know with every fiber of my being that she didn't jump.

"You pushed my baby sister off the pier." I finally say the words I've been choking down all these months as I sat across from him in my office.

"What? No, I didn't. You're insane."

"I am that." A rueful chuckle falls off my lips. "But my memory is crystal clear."

Isaac barks a laugh, as if he's just heard the most absurd joke. "Where? When?"

"When we were sixteen. In Santa Cruz. She left her shift early at the ice cream shop—"

"Oh. That night. I heard about that. I wasn't there—"

"You were. I saw you."

His eyebrow arches as his mouth presses into a thin line. A flicker of awareness crosses his gaze. He remembers. I know he does.

"Sophie took my early shift at Norm's that night—remember the ice cream shop on the wharf? We both worked there that summer. She took my shift, so she got off early and I had to close. Do you remember what you said to me that day?" Isaac shakes his head, so I continue. "You told me you still loved Brianna, that you were getting back together with her. You broke up with me and took Brianna to the wharf that night for a date."

Isaac remains silent, an apathetic look on his face.

"Sophie saw you when she left work. She followed you because she wanted to talk to you—to tell you how you broke my heart . . . And then you shoved her. You must have gotten in a fight and—"

"No, that's not what happened."

"Liar," I spit. "Fucking *liar*."

"I'm not—"

"Brianna told me—"

His eyes widen. "Brianna told you what? You talked to Brianna about this? When?"

I clamp down on my lips, realizing I've revealed too much. "She walked me through what happened. She said you thought Sophie was me, that it was only meant to be a prank."

Isaac's nostrils flare like an angry animal, but he doesn't say anything.

"Just tell me why. Why did you do it?"

"I didn't." He growls. "I swear, Shae."

My name from his mouth causes ice to form in my veins. I hate him. I love him. The pain of what he did to me then and now is palpable, so real I can taste it like bile rising in my throat. "Don't fucking lie to me."

My eyes flash around the room until they land on a hammer nearby. I stand, crossing the space to a small workbench that sits in the corner, and grab the hammer off the surface. "Every time you tell a lie, I'm taking off a finger, starting with your ring finger. It's not like you know what it means to be faithful anyway." I cast my eyes to the wedding band on his left hand. "You're living a lie."

"So are you," he shoots back.

I nearly growl my anger at him. "Hardly. I've only told a few white lies to balance the scales of justice."

"Tell yourself what you need to, crazy bitch."

I suck air through my teeth at his assault. Seething, I pull the hammer back, prepared to smash his hand—anything to force him to live inside of the pain that he's caused.

"Wait!" He moves his bound hands to cover his face. "I'll tell you exactly what happened that night if you tell me where I can find Brianna."

"No," I growl. "It's not like I can trust anything you say anyway."

His eyes turn an inky black shade, almost reminding me of that dark, hooded look that descends over them right before he fucks me.

"I swear, I'll tell you everything."

"You're going to anyway, or I'm taking off your fingers one at a time." I flip the hammer in my palm playfully, swinging the clawed end closer and closer to his forehead as I do. He flinches every time the weapon nears him, but he never breaks my gaze. He's fuming quietly; his teeth are clenched, and his jaw tenses with anger. He wants to kill me. Finally, we are on equal footing.

"I'll tell you whatever you think you need to hear," he grits out.

I blink, the intensity of his dark irises unnerving me. Like he's the one who's flipped a switch and become something else, something wild to be feared. Isaac is smart. The only thing sharper than his tongue is his mind. I've learned that by listening to him in his therapy sessions. He excels in business because he thinks three steps ahead of everyone else and remains in complete control of his world, which is why it's so unsettling to have him here, lying at my feet and begging for mercy.

"Start from the beginning." I hiss.

He gulps. "From what I can remember . . . Brianna thought it was you spying on us. She was so angry, so jealous. I told her to ignore you, but—"

"But it wasn't me—"

"It was dark, especially on the last pier. There wasn't a soul out there with us, so when Brianna saw the Norm's shirt, she just assumed—"

"Fucking bitch," I snarl, realizing I've had it all wrong this entire time. "How do I know you're telling the truth?"

"You don't. But does it matter?"

"Of course. Justice matters." I blink away a memory of paramedics walking my sister's lifeless body up the beach on a stretcher.

Seaweed clung to her hair and wrapped around her neck. She'd been in the water for only a few hours, and her face was bloated and a sickly shade of gray.

"Brianna wanted to talk to you. I hung back, thinking you would have closure if you could speak to Brianna—"

"Closure?" I laugh. "You were a coward, then and now."

He shrugs. "Whatever. I don't know what happened next. Brianna told me it was an accident. I didn't see anything."

"Liar."

"It was dark," he offers simply.

"Why didn't you call the police if you knew what happened?"

"Brianna said she would," he says.

"So, your conscience is clear, then?" Frustrated tears spark to life behind my eyelids.

"As clear as yours." He smiles. "Or maybe yours isn't clear. Maybe that's why you're really here. Maybe you caused your sister's death when you switched that shift with her. Or when you let her leave to chase Brianna and me down that night to defend you—"

"No. I didn't know she was going after you. I didn't—how could I be to blame?"

"It was just an accident, Shae. It's better for all of us if we believe that and move on. There's no way to prove otherwise. Don't you think it's time we put this to bed? Have you really let this torture you for all these years?" He huffs. "Jesus, you told yourself a lie all this time, and now you're exacting revenge for it?"

I swallow the ball of pain in my throat. Is he right? I can't tell anymore.

I squeeze my eyes closed, willing a million long-buried thoughts to resurface in the hopes of finding a glimmer of truth among the murky memories.

My father's tears when officers confirmed my sister's body had been found.

Newspaper headlines reporting the death of a local teenager, with suicide as a suspected cause.

Her funeral. Her burial. Her life lost. My good half gone.

"Tell me where Brianna is," he commands.

I blink away the nightmare memories. "I can't talk about this anymore tonight." I drop the hammer at his feet and stand. "If you want your freedom so badly, take off a thumb. I promise, if you do it, there'll be less blood than if you make me do it." I smile leisurely and then step over him to go up the stairs. "In fact, let's make a deal. You take off a finger, and I'll tell you where your girl is."

"Shae, stop."

My smirk deepens as I climb the stairs.

"Shae!"

I reach the top stair and turn to wave once before flicking off the basement light, leaving him in complete darkness.

"Shae! Fuck! Come back!"

I slam the basement door and give Isaac's dog a scratch under the chin before swiping an unopened bottle of champagne off the counter. I tuck my Rohypnol-laced whiskey under my arm and then close Isaac's front door, careful to be sure it's locked behind me, Isaac's fading screams already lost to my ears.

CHAPTER 34

"I brought donuts!" I sing out as I enter Isaac's kitchen the next morning. His dog greets me with a raspy bark and a wagging tail. It strikes me then that I don't even know the dog's name. I think Isaac told me at one point, but I can't remember it now. Seems like an oversight, considering how well Isaac and I have gotten to know each other over the months. "Hey, buddy."

The dog licks my hand and then scoops his leash in his mouth and brings it to me. Damn. He must need to go outside. I sigh, set the bag of jelly-filled donuts on the counter, and then attach the leash to the dog's collar. I take him to the back door. I find that the backyard is private, with towering hedges and flowering fruit trees lining the sharply manicured lawn. Everything about their life is picture-perfect. Funny how, just beneath the surface, their lives are anything but. The dog pauses to do his business under a lemon tree before he looks up at me, eyes wide and tongue hanging from his mouth.

"Hmm, I bet you want a treat now, don't you?" When I say the word *treat*, he pauses, eyes alert. We walk back into the kitchen, and the dog leads me right to the pantry. I open the door wide, my gaze landing on a bag of bacon-flavored dog treats. I scoop a few from the bag and toss them at the dog. He gobbles them up and then moves to his water bowl, where he spends a long minute drinking.

"Okay, now that you're taken care of, let's see about your owner." I shut the pantry door and swing the basement one wide. Darkness and silence cling to every nook. I flip the light on to find the spot where I left Isaac last night is vacant. "Guess he's been up to something."

I take the steps slowly, aware that I left the hammer within Isaac's reach when I went home last night. Maybe he took my advice and lopped off a thumb to free himself. A dark chuckle leaves my lips before I can stop it. I descend the stairs quietly, Isaac's dog following me down. When I reach the bottom step, I pause, taking in the empty space. "Hello?"

Silence greets me.

Isaac's dog trots around the corner of the stairs and out of sight. I suck in a breath and then follow him. Once I move a few steps around the stairwell, I find that the dog has curled up next to Isaac's motionless form. "Isaac?"

I step closer, checking for any sign of life. The hammer sits next to his left thigh, and all ten of his fingers are intact. Guess the coward didn't take my advice after all. I'd half hoped he would just do it to save me from the bloodbath that will result if I have to handle things.

I bend, poking at his arm. "Hey—"

He jerks awake, bright-green eyes suddenly on me. He doesn't say a word, but his eyes say more than enough.

"Morning. I brought donuts." I offer a smile.

He still doesn't reply, but his stare is unwavering. His dog stands, turns, and begins licking Isaac's bound wrists. They're red and bruised; it's clear he's been trying to escape his binds, to no avail.

Annoyance bubbles to life inside me at his stubborn silence. "Opted to keep your thumbs, huh?"

He huffs, pets his dog with one palm, and then drops his gaze from mine.

"I fucking tried. I can't hold onto the hammer with my wrists tied like this. Anyway, I thought if I told you the truth, you'd let me go," he says.

I pause, letting his words linger as he continues to pet the dog. "I let him outside to go to the bathroom when I got here. And gave him treats when he was finished. He's a good boy."

Isaac's gaze bores into mine. "What are we talking about here?"

I shut my mouth, unsure of what to say.

"Seriously, I gave you what you wanted—the truth. What else are you looking for?" His eyes sparkle with dark amusement. "Do you think we're in a relationship or something? We fucked a few times. Nothing more. You need to get over it."

I gulp down his harsh words, each one cutting like a razor. "It's not about that."

"Then what is it about? For fuck's sake, you won't even tell me where my wife is!"

"Because I don't know," I offer.

"I don't fucking believe you," he says through gritted teeth. "I thought if I told you what happened that night, you'd tell me more about Brianna."

"What do you need me to tell you? She's been texting you. If she wanted you to know, she'd tell you herself."

He shakes his head as if he doesn't believe a word I'm saying. His instincts are on point; I'll give him that.

"Revenge, then? Is this just some crackpot plan for revenge twenty years later?"

I digest his statement and then finally reply, "I appreciate the truth, if I can even trust you, but that doesn't absolve you. You're still a bad person. You still need someone to teach—"

Before I can finish my sentence, Isaac launches himself at me, his bound arms circling my neck and yanking me to him in a violent embrace. He smells so good. That's all I can think as he attempts to choke the life out of me. This is his fatal flaw, I realize. He's impulsive and irrational and underestimates my sheer determination to make him hurt. My desire to inflict pain on this man is so strong, I can taste it.

"Let me go, and I'll tell you about your wife."

He does instantly, unwrapping me from his grasp and sliding away from me. His dog follows him and sits between Isaac's spread thighs. It's as if he's protecting his owner, but in reality, it's the world that needs protecting from Isaac. Just like an apex predator, Isaac is ever the opportunist. He's trained himself to identify weakness and attack when it suits him. He takes no prisoners—I am evidence of that. Brianna too, now that I've seen what he's like when his wife is missing.

"Tell me where she is," he demands.

"I told you already. I don't know where she is right now."

"When's the last time you saw her?" he asks.

I shrug. "We met at the country club a while back. I haven't seen her since then."

"Have you talked to her?"

I shake my head.

"Not even for video sessions?"

I don't answer him, unsure of how much to reveal. I finally say, "I'll tell you"—his eyes narrow with annoyance—"*after* you take off your ring finger."

"What the fuck—"

"If you wait for me to do it, I'll take off every single one of them. *Slowly.*" I shoot him a sweet smile. "Hard to play golf without fingers, right?"

He groans, green eyes closing. His dog nuzzles into his chest, as if he knows the personal anguish his owner is in. I wonder if Isaac's ever shown tenderness to another soul the way this dog is comforting him right now.

"Listen, all is not lost. Take off your ring finger, and I'll let you keep it. If you think you can drive yourself to the emergency room, they'll sew it right back on for you. Like brand-new. *Mostly.*"

"Why are you doing this?"

"Because you fucking broke me." I grasp the hammer, and the strength to smash his skull wells inside me. "I need my pound of flesh." I swing the hammer at his thigh. It lands with a soft thud, and he yells with the burst of brutal pain. "My official diagnosis is that you're obstinate and unbearable—using people as objects like a spoiled man-child. I thought inserting myself in your marriage would be enough, but it wasn't. It only made me realize that you're both narcissistic assholes who stole the only thing that mattered from me and then moved on with your perfect lives as if none of it even happened. As if we didn't even exist." I swing the hammer in his direction. "Do it."

He squints, face contorted with the perceived pain of my command. "I can't with my hands tied."

I narrow my eyes and then glance at the workbench. I stand, crossing the room to grab needle-nose pliers. I pull the package of zip ties from my pocket and nod at him to follow me to the bench. He does, his dog following dutifully along with us. When Isaac reaches the edge of the bench, I loop one of his wrists with the leg of the bench and tighten the tie. He groans when the plastic cuts into his flesh. I use the pliers to cut the other zip tie, so now, only one of his wrists is bound, the other free.

"There you go." My smile is wide when I toss him the hammer. He catches it in one hand with a scowl.

He stares so intently at me it looks like he might enjoy extracting my windpipe with the claws of the hammer. "You promise to let me go and tell me where she is?"

I nod politely.

Quickly, before I'm even ready, he swings the clawed end at the ring finger on his bound hand. Upon impact, he growls, and blood spurts and pools between his fingers. The spot where his ring finger once was gushes blood and has turned an unnatural shade of white. His dog whines, attempts to sniff at the wound, but not before Isaac pulls away, swiping his own severed finger into his palm. "Could you get me a fucking towel, at least?"

I swipe a dirty rag off the workbench and toss it his way. And then I dig in the pocket of my jeans, pull out a phone, and toss it at him. "There you are."

He struggles to lift the phone with blood gushing from his wound, but when he finally does, the screen comes alive. A photo of Isaac and Brianna in formal attire kissing passionately on the beach is revealed. His own blood makes a mess of the screen. His features morph into a cringe as if I've landed a hammer blow to his heart. He does love her, I think for the first time. He's just been hiding it well. Isaac is the kind of man who believes love is weakness. It's too bad; if he'd been the kind of warm and empathetic man the world needs, he wouldn't be here now, at the whim of my next hammer swing.

"Take off another finger, and I'll tell you about the last time I saw her." His gorgeous features crush into a look of unbearable pain.

"Dealer's choice." I nod to his bloody hand, indicating that he's welcome to choose the next finger he's willing to part with.

He gulps, emotion welling in his eyes before he swings the hammer again and severs his pinkie finger. It hangs by a few thin threads of flesh. The sight of his pain causes a wave of warmth to envelop me. A slow smile stretches my lips before I finally say, "You're good at following instructions." I repeat the thing he said to me the first time we had sex. "The last time I saw your wife was six weeks ago when we left the country club."

Brianna's perfect smile, lined with pearly-white designer teeth, comes to mind.

"And then what?" he growls, attempting to hold the blood-soaked rag to his newest wound.

"See for yourself." I gesture to Brianna's cell phone in his lap. He groans, then swipes at the screen with his mangled hand. "Check the messages." He does, and when his gaze lands on her text messages, his eyes squeeze closed with the realization. "I've been texting you on her behalf."

"S-she's—" He can't finish his sentence because hot tears clog his throat and flow down his cheeks.

"Check the photos."

He sobs, sucks in a breath of air, and then fumbles with his thumb on the screen. I know the moment he sees it. The single photo I took of Brianna that day. I know every pixel by heart because I've studied the photo every night before bed for over a month. He drops the bloody phone in his lap, and I can't help the smile that lights my face.

There she is. Slumped over a fallen pine, bare feet in the sand, body lifeless with a head wound that seeps maroon. The sand under her head is soaked with her blood, and the moonlight cuts slivers of light over her floral summer dress. One Prada flat lies next to her head. She's beautiful, elegant, even in death.

"She's dead," he finally murmurs through the tears. "This entire time . . . it's been you texting me? It was all a lie?"

"Oh, don't be dramatic. All of life is a lie. Your marriage is an illusion. This place is. We're all living a lie every day, pretending to get along with a smile." I enjoy seeing him like this, weak and at my mercy, so I continue. "You were right to question the Rosemary Beach picture." I grin. "I photoshopped it. Brianna would never spend time in Rosemary Beach, too . . . ordinary and pedestrian, right? I know that now. Brianna is so pretentious, it's fucking unbearable—a West Coast girl to the core. I'm pretty proud of my photoshop skills though." A sweet smile curves my lips. "You thought she was in paradise, but really, she was rotting at the bottom of the ocean."

Isaac's tears come harder now, and I realize this was the moment I was waiting for—to see his pain as acutely as I felt it the day he stole my sister. I never thought I'd see this man show emotion, and I wonder if this is the first time he ever has, his life bubble-wrapped from hardship in all the years before now.

"She got what she deserved," I state. "A watery grave just like my sister."

CHAPTER 35

"You know what Brianna told me before she died?" I offer as some small means of solace. "She said *Isaac isn't all he'd have you believe.* I know what she means now. I should have heeded her warning then. Hindsight is twenty-twenty, right?" I giggle as I look down at Isaac.

"Please just let me go—"

"You know, for a while, I loved you enough to overlook the real you. But not anymore. I'm sure I'll live to regret not killing you." I caress his cheek with my palm. "But I love you more."

"Please, Shae—whatever you want. Fuck, I'll take off my fucking hand if that's what it takes."

"Mm, love when you beg." A smirk lifts my cheeks. "I can't tell you how many times I'll hear you begging for your life in my dreams, like music to my ears. Wanna know what the last thing your wife said was before I crushed her skull with a rock?"

He shakes his head, eyes closed as if he's trying to will himself out of this predicament.

"Nothing. She said nothing because she never saw me coming. That's another one of my regrets. I should have taken her out head-on, just to see the awareness of her mistake in her eyes. The fear . . .

it's intoxicating. That's why people kill—the scent of fear, the adrenaline. I think I'm addicted."

His mouth is clamped closed, as if defeat has finally subdued him. His skin is turning a sickly shade of white. For the first time, I think if he doesn't get medical help soon, he might bleed out right here in front of me.

But I'm not ready for the torture to end. Not yet.

"I'll probably live to regret this, but despite everything, I think I love you too much to kill you. First love leaves a mark, ya know?" He doesn't respond, so I continue. "I think I'll just leave you here with the mutt." I glance at his dog sitting patiently at his hip. "He's loyal. Maybe I should leave your fate in his paws." I giggle at my own joke. "We'll see how loyal man's best friend is once he gets hungry, huh?" Isaac still doesn't respond. I wonder if his mind has already shut down, shock settling in. I'm suddenly bored with this scene, and the thick scent of Isaac's blood in the air is turning my stomach. Isaac's dog whines, wags his tail, and looks up at me once. He would be a nice souvenir, even better than a photo of the mangled mess this man has been reduced to at my feet.

"On second thought, he's too precious to leave behind, I think." I smile, tapping my thigh for the dog to follow me. He pauses, attempts to make eye contact with his owner, and then gives up when he gets no response. "Come on, puppy."

The dog wags his tail, takes a few steps in my direction, pauses to glance at Isaac once more, and then follows me up the stairs dutifully. So much for loyalty, I snicker. Once we reach the kitchen, I hook the leash to his collar, and without another word, we walk out the front door and into our future. I wonder if Isaac will pass the lie detector test when police begin investigating his wife's disappearance. He will be the most likely suspect when they finally find her body. The husband always is. I grin to myself as I think that, finally, I've taken back my power.

It takes me just a few minutes to make my way down the street to my cottage. By the time we reach it, my mind is spinning with the implications of the mess I've found myself in. I couldn't bring myself to kill Isaac. But on some level, I'm hoping he's dead by the time he's found, and then authorities will assume this was a murder-suicide.

I'm not sure what my next move will be, but staying here and using Kelly's name is no longer an option. We reach the cottage, and I let the dog off his leash to roam the fenced-in backyard. My cell-phone rings to life. The call is unknown, so I let it go to voicemail. Just as I'm about to head back into the cottage, Taylor sends me a wave over the fence.

"Shit," I whisper as I wave back.

"Got a new dog?" Taylor bends to pet Isaac's dog over the fence.

"Just dog-sitting," I offer.

"Oh, fun. What's his name?"

I pause because I don't know this dog's fucking name. "Um—"

"What's this?" Taylor pauses, holding the dog's chin in both palms to get a better look at something. "Is this blood?"

"Oh, he caught a squirrel on our walk."

Taylor doesn't seem to be paying any attention to me. My heart thunders like a drum in my ears as I realize Taylor is smarter and more observant than I've been giving him credit for.

Taylor has been watching this entire time. My neighbor, the nosy witness.

"I have to make a few phone calls. Let's catch up later though." I throw him a half wave. Taylor still doesn't acknowledge me, his sole focus on the stupid dog. I shut the sliding door, locking it behind me for good measure. I have to think fast. I shouldn't have brought the dog home with me. I should have just snuck back into the cottage quietly, packed my most important things, and then hit the road. To where, I'm still not sure. And now I'm out of time. A chill of awareness runs through me as I realize that even the little I spoke to Taylor over these last months was too much. I imagine investigators knocking on his door to ask a few questions about the unfortunate death of his neighbor, and the first thing he'll tell them is that he saw me fucking the victim on my balcony just a few weeks ago.

My phone chimes with a new voicemail, and without thinking I check the message. Thirty seconds of heavy breathing is all I can hear, before a voice mumbles, "I'm coming for you."

A groan falls from my lips as I hang up and climb the stairs two at a time. I have to leave, my time is up in Carmel. Thankfully, I like to keep a duffel handy in the closet packed with a few overnight things and my most precious items—the locket my mom left me before she vanished from my life, all of Kelly's essential identification items like her passport and information for various bank accounts, and lastly, the stack of files and notebooks Kelly kept on me all these years. I haven't worked my way through all of them yet.

I've been so distracted the last several weeks with Isaac and Brianna, I haven't had any time to reach deep into the vault of client notes still waiting for me. Truth be told, it was hard to read all her thoughts about me over the last years. Her support was unwavering with each session we had, and I suppose it was foolish of me to think she wasn't holding back her real thoughts. Kelly spent pages and pages dissecting our interactions after each session—far above and beyond a normal therapist.

I chuckle to myself as I wonder if therapists are supposed to pick a favorite. Maybe playing favorites on the therapist's couch isn't quite the same as a mother choosing a favorite child, but I confess, I did kind of feel that way. Kelly spent hours on the phone with me in the early years as I broke down into an incoherent mess, my moods flying from manic to suicidal in the span of moments.

Thankfully, those days have passed because Kelly helped me find the right medication to stabilize my mood swings so we could get to the heart of the trauma that infected my brain. I think of the hours we spent discussing the years of neglect and torture I suffered at the hands of the people who raised me.

I bite back tears, trying to shove away the memories of nights locked in my bedroom closet, the smell of urine stinging my nose as I heard them scream insults and throw things at each other until the police had to be called.

I swipe the notebook I'd been reading off the nightstand, tossing it on the top of the duffel. It falls open to the last page, where I see a small stack of old papers folded into the built-in pocket. Kelly's familiar chicken scratch, not unlike my own, is on the outside of the envelope. I pull it fully out of the pocket and frown when a single phrase stands out among the others. ***Birth Certificate.*** Shallow breaths escape me as I slide the envelope open and untuck a tattered green paper from the pocket.

Baby Name: Shae Bianca Miller
Birth Date: August 8, 1989
Mother: KellyAnne O'Reilly
Father: Robert Miller

I shove the birth certificate back into the envelope as tears spill down my cheeks. This is *my* birth certificate. I can't make sense of what I'm looking at—the truth spelled out in ink, the kind of truth that tears worlds apart. How long had she known? Every session, every seemingly heartfelt conversation—was it all a facade?

My hands tremble with a cocktail of betrayal and shock. No wonder Kelly—*my mom*—was so relentless in her therapeutic pursuits with me. She wasn't just trying to help a troubled client; she was trying to amend her failures as a mother. But why keep it a secret? Why the lies? The deception makes my skin crawl, and the room feels like it's closing in on me.

"Why didn't you tell me?" I whisper into the emptiness of my room, half-expecting the walls to answer. The silence that follows is suffocating. Each session under her care, every moment she pushed me to open up about my darkest fears and painful memories—it all feels tainted now. Was any of her empathy real, or was I just a project to her? A way to ease her guilt?

I feel a cold laugh bubble up, bitter and mocking. A ruse. It had to be. How could it not be? Yet, as I sit here, surrounded by the debris of what I once thought was a genuine connection, a shred of guilt pierces through the anger. Maybe I lashed out back at the psychiatric hospital when I shoved the hot coals in her face, the pain and rage of years of abandonment channeled into a single moment of fury. I'd hurt her, maimed her for life, striking back at a therapist who failed me in my moment of need. But she was my mother. The mother who abandoned Sophie and me.

The thought of Sophie twists the knife deeper. If Kelly hadn't left, if she'd been the mother we needed, would Sophie still be alive? The questions gnaw at me, relentless and cruel. They fuel a dark, smoldering anger that no amount of therapy could ever reach.

The need for answers, for closure—propels me forward. I need to see her, to confront her, even if she can't respond. I need to stand before her and ask why. Why leave us? Why hide behind a therapist's notebook? Did you ever truly care, or was I just your penance?

As I grab my keys, the weight of the decision settles on my shoulders. This isn't just a trip to visit my mom; it's a journey to confront the ghost that has haunted my entire life. Each mile will be a step through the past, a past filled with shadows and questions that might never get answers.

I have to believe that confronting her will offer some form of cathartic release. Maybe then, I can start to untangle the web of lies and maybe—just maybe—I can start to forgive, not for her sake, but for mine. Without forgiveness, without some semblance of understanding, I'll be trapped in this cycle of anger and hurt forever.

I shove everything into the duffel and then zip it and make my way down the stairs. I stop in my office and toss the photo of Sophie and me in my bag, then pause in the kitchen and glance out to the backyard. Taylor is gone, so I open the door and call Isaac's dog—he trots up and I grab the leash. I glance once more around the small space before stepping out the front door and heading for the car. I put the dog in the backseat, slide behind the wheel, and toss the duffel in the passenger seat beside me, and then turn the key in the ignition.

"Well, off to our next adventure," I say to the dog. "It's time for a little reunion. And you're gonna need a name, huh buddy?" He catches my eye in the rearview mirror and I swear I almost see a smile on his little doggy face. "You look like a . . . Toby." I smile back at my new companion. "Do you like that? We had a beagle named Toby when I was little, he was such a good boy. Toby has a nice ring to it, don't you think?"

Toby's smile seems to deepen and I take it as a sign of acceptance. I back out of the driveway slowly, pausing a moment to think of the utter destruction I've caused to the neighborhood in just a few short months. I'm capable of inflicting more damage than I realized. From

Brianna, battered and sinking to the bottom of the Pacific with an old fisherman's anchor tied at her ankle, to Isaac, left to rot in his own bungalow's basement.

At what point does a dream become a nightmare? Like love, does it happen slowly and then all at once? I think of the years of abuse I endured after my sister died, me the last girl standing to take my father's stones and arrows. I survived him, but barely. He ran off everyone else in my life. Well, I thought he did.

Until now. Until Kelly.

EPILOGUE

"Hello?" I call out as I enter the condo. The click of Toby's nails follows me in.

Sickly silence clings to everything. A pair of old Crocs sit by the door, as if their owner might walk up any minute to slip them on and run errands. But not here, not now, not yet.

I take a few more cautious steps down the hall in search of any signs of life. The decor is sparse—like a model house—not yet made into a home. I continue on soft steps, reaching the kitchen to find it devoid of life. No bananas on the counter, no stack of mail or even a dirty glass in the sink. It's as if the ghost of a person lives here, but then, I guess that would make sense, considering the circumstances.

A quick glance around the kitchen reveals a small cache of medication, some pain meds and antidepressants and more I'm not familiar with. All of them are prescribed to Shae Halston. A shiver runs through me, seeing how many meds I'm currently on. Well, the old me, anyway.

I snort-laugh at how well and truly fucked I left Kelly near the kiln at the psychiatric hospital that day. It's been nearly two years since then. What a reunion this will be, and the best part, it will be one-sided. Kelly won't recognize me. I'm not Shae anymore—maybe I never was. Shae Halston came with a lifetime's worth of trauma and baggage that nearly sank her. But I'm not Kelly Fraser either. I'm a new hybrid person. The woman I've become is unrecognizable.

I pat my pocket, feeling the trifolded piece of paper I've been carrying around for the last week. The tie that binds us. It took me a few days to track down Kelly, but knowing she wouldn't be far from the last inpatient hospital she was at in Pismo Beach gave me a general area where to cast my net. After that, I called the hospital, impersonating the home-care nurse assigned to her case, requesting copies of her discharge papers to be faxed to me. The receptionist at the hospital seemed put out that I was asking her to do her job. I apologized profusely, claiming a clerical error on the part of the company I worked for, and then I was in. Two days ago, I learned that Kelly—under the name Shae Halston—has rented a tiny condo only a few blocks from the beach. I'm still shocked she—or me— was released from her sentence after just two years. Apparently, they deemed her incapacitated by her injuries enough to be harmless to the general public, but what they didn't anticipate was the real me, returning to finish what I started.

Kelly alive is a risk to my very life. I doubt she'll ever be able to speak again after the damage I did to her, but with physical therapy and advances in medical technology, there is always a chance. I tucked what I have left of the Rohypnol into my duffel before I bailed on Carmel. I don't think I'll have to use it again, but just knowing it's an option gives me comfort. I imagine all of the prescription medications Kelly is on will be enough to keep her docile and under my control, however long I decide to stay here. This little reunion of ours is just a quick layover before I decide my next move—Malibu or La Jolla, maybe.

I continue to poke my way around Kelly's new condo. I stumble across a stack of rental paperwork, my name listed as the renter. I think for the first time that maybe I should start calling her Shae in my mind. It might make things easier over the coming days. I'm not at all sure of Kelly's current state. Can she walk? Has speech therapy made her at least partially verbal? Does she have the use of her hands? Does she eat via a feeding tube? I have so many questions. I guess I won't know until I know.

I pass the living area and find it empty. No signs of life anywhere. I continue to move through the space, thinking for the first time that maybe she's at a doctor's appointment today with her current home-care nurse. I spent the last two days plotting how best to handle this developing situation. I'd mistakenly assumed that Kelly would be in the state's custody for the rest of her life after the criminal case relating to Jesika's death and Dean's injuries, but I guess the state is at capacity for crazy people. Anyway, how could Kelly hurt anyone again when, last I saw her, she couldn't even get out of bed? I should have known hurting Kelly would only be a temporary fix. It was shortsighted of me to think I wouldn't have to come finish the job I started.

I pass the bathroom and then pause when I hear it—the telltale *beep-beep-beep* of a medical device. My veins sizzle with heat as I approach the bedroom. This is it. The moment where my past and future meet. I still haven't fully processed what I saw on the birth certificate. The truth of it unnerves me to my core. I want to believe it's a misprint, a misunderstanding, easily explained by some unknown fact that eludes me.

Sucking in a deep breath, I turn the corner of the bedroom quietly and then nearly stumble the rest of the way into the room when I see her. She naps upright in her home hospital bed. She's aged—her dry skin sags, and she looks like she hasn't seen sunshine in years. I guess she probably hasn't, considering she's been confined to a bed in a medically induced coma for most of that time.

Now that she sleeps, I can take time to study her face. Her features are different—everything familiar about her has changed after repeated skin grafts to repair her burned skin. Her eyes are stretched into uneven almonds. The new skin molded around her nose is shiny and pink, an indication that her flesh is still healing. She looks like the victim of a house fire . . . or a pile of coals to the face. It's odd seeing someone who existed so powerfully in my mind completely incapacitated, a shell of a human. I thought, on some level, I would be happy to see her, but I'm not. Especially even more so now that I know this woman walked away from me during the most important time of my life.

Kelly sighs in her sleep, shifts minutely, and then a gentle wave of snores falls from her lips. She's so peaceful. And I've come to shatter her world.

"Fucking gold-digging bitch!" My father's voice sends splinters of terror through me. He's angry. Right on time. Most of the days of the week it's like this—peaceful until five p.m. And then, depending on the kind of day he's had, spiteful raging or an oppressive surliness pervades every nook and cranny. Even hidden in my second-floor closet, there is no escape.

Sophie clings to me just like always. She's only three, but already she knows real terror. I think of my friends and the back-and-forth relationships they have with their siblings, but not me. I hardly remember a time when Sophie wasn't clinging to me with tears in her eyes. I wanted to resent her presence in my life, but how could I when she was terrorized as well and truly as I was? Most kids are bullied and brutalized by other kids, but not us. By the time I was old enough to go to kindergarten— my first escape—I knew there was no bigger bully than my father.

I'd found the only escape for us was here—hidden among polka-dot summer skort sets and outgrown kids shoes. Surrounded by tiny things, we did our best to disappear. I used to pray that they'd forget us. Maybe it would just slip their minds that we were even here. After all, how important could we be if they could abuse and neglect us to the brink of death?

"My sweet girls." The closet door swings open, and suddenly, my mother is there, a halo of evening light surrounding her. "Gimme hugs. I'm going away for a little while."

Sophie and I remain silent. Silence is the only thing that keeps us safe. We've learned the hard way.

Our mother crouches, hauls us into her arms, and squeezes tightly. She rubs Sophie's back as tears well in her eyes. When she turns to me, I only stare. A frown flickers over her face before she clasps my cheeks between her palms and looks me directly in the eye. "Be good girls for your daddy, okay? I know it's hard, but you are brave and bold and strong. I'll be back for you—I promise."

Tears threaten to choke off my air supply, but I don't cry. I never cry.

"I love you, girls." She plants a kiss on my forehead and whispers, "Take care of Sophie while I'm gone, okay?"

That's the last memory I have of my mother.

Until now.

"Hello, Mom."

My eternal gratitude to my editor, Lisa, at *Silently Correcting Your Grammar*. Your patience with me knows no bounds and I am so thankful!

To my dearest friend, Nelle Lamarr: Your passion for storytelling and persistent work ethic are constant inspirations! Thank you for your friendship over the last decade—the day we met at The Naughty Mafia book signing in Las Vegas in 2013 changed my life! Our travel shenanigans and champagne and giggles make my world go 'round!

Steve DeJonge—my favorite weirdo! Thank you for making me smile, especially on the bad days. Our crazy conversations always make me think outside the box and the way you show up with so much love for the people in your life inspires me to be better. You're a special kind of soul and I'm honored that you've been so open with me over the course of our friendship.

Adrienne Jamail—our friendship feels like it was written in the stars! Our conversations always leave me feeling inspired and fulfilled. Thank you for loving, lifting up, and sparking the souls of women!

Ames Goldman—I live for our soul-stirring conversations and your hugs! You're such a bright light and I always feel so lucky when you choose to shine it on me. Keep writing, keep smiling, and keep loving. The world needs more of you.

I'm so lucky to call the always flirty and sometimes insane baristas at Aldea Coffee friends—you bring joy to my day in ways I can't even begin to express! I feel like I've found a little slice of home at the coffee shop and it feeds my soul and provides an endless stream of wild inspiration!

For my family—you fill my heart with the kind of love I didn't know was possible. Thank you for your patience while I play with the characters in my head all day.

And to my favorite people on the planet: book people! I'm so honored to be a part of such a supportive community of readers and book lovers. Without your support, I wouldn't have the courage to write a single sentence. You're the wind beneath my wings! If you're ever in West Michigan, send me an email (info@adrianeleigh.com) and I'll take you out for coffee at Aldea!

xo A

ABOUT THE AUTHOR

Adriane Leigh is the *USA Today*–bestselling author of multiple novels and novellas, some of which have been translated into French, Spanish, Italian, and Portuguese. Her work has appeared in publications such as *Vogue* magazine and the *Montreal Gazette*. Leigh also founded RARE: Romance Author & Reader Events, a community that organizes book conventions around the world. She lives on Lake Michigan with her family.

FOR A GOOD TIME

follow us on our socials

podiumentertainment.com

@podiumentertainment

/podiumentertainment

@podium_ent

@podiumentertainment